Vivie Goes to Hell in a Hatchback

A Supernatural Action/Adventure

Sherrill WARK

crowecreations.ca
Ottawa Canada

Vivie Goes to Hell in a Hatchback
Copyright © 2019 by Sherrill Wark

First Crowe Creations edition July 2019

Designed by Crowe Creations
Text set in Times New Roman; headings set in Crazy Girls Blond BTN

Cover photo from iStock: bobbieo, ID:108269186.
Cover design © 2019 by Crowe Creations

Crowe Creations
ISBN: 978-1-998831-22-7

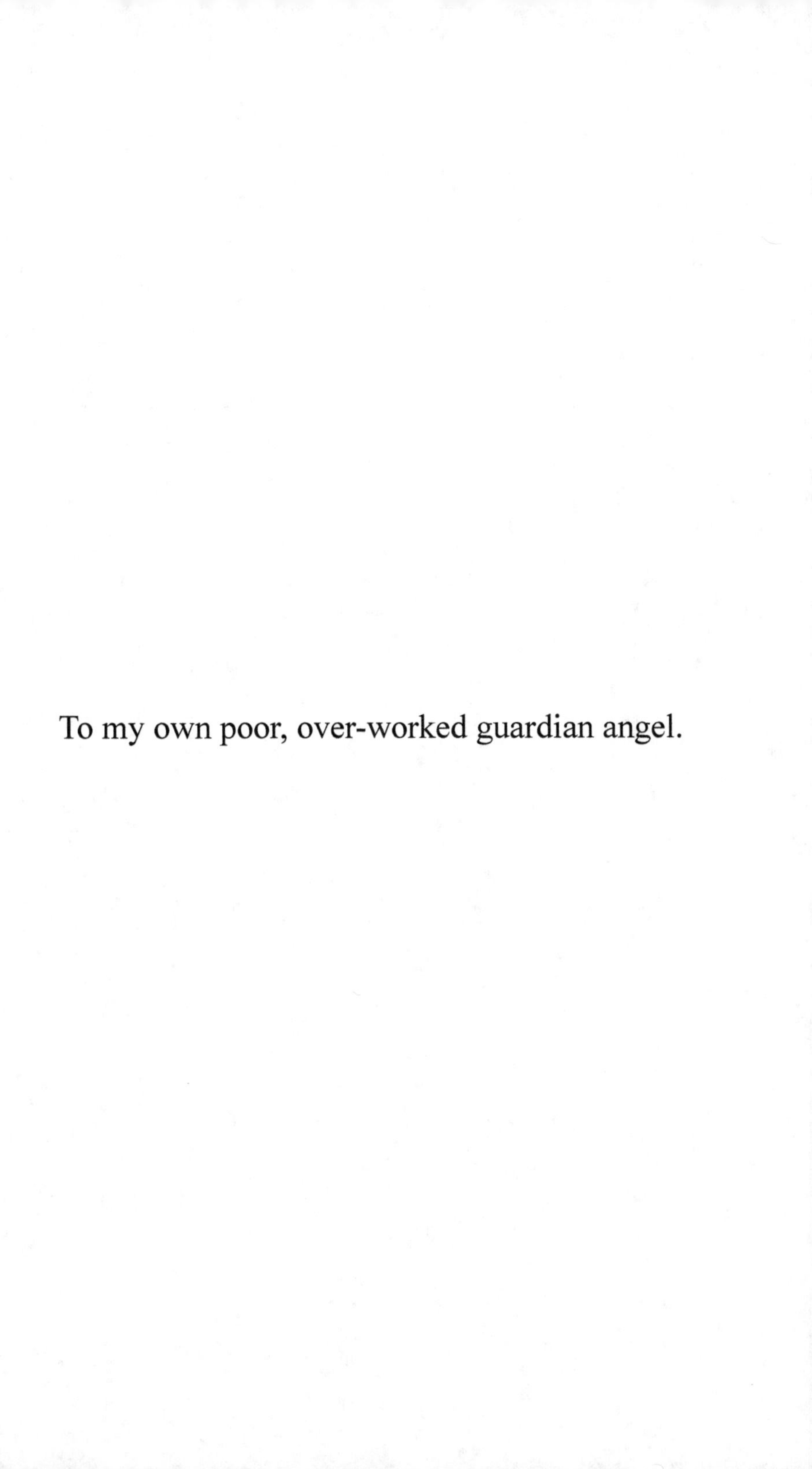

To my own poor, over-worked guardian angel.

"Fasten your seatbelts."—Bette Davis as
Margo Channing in *All About Eve*

One

OOPS. THAT DIDN'T WORK OUT so great, did it? I heard Pete's voice in the back of my head like my Little Voice must have sounded to Vivie many times: something to be ignored.

His name wasn't Pete but that's what we called him, mostly me, because he was such a know-it-all: bow tie, clipboard, tapping pen, bossy beyond bossy. It was short for Saint Peter, the guy who meets us at the Pearly Gates, so they say, although I doubt the real Saint Peter carries a clipboard. Our Pete's real name was Trevor. And Saint Peter he wasn't. But this wasn't the time to be pondering over Trevor a.k.a. Pete. My Charge had just plastered herself against a cement overpass support. This was beyond embarrassing.

I tried to tell her, but she had her music cranked up so loud it's a wonder the glass hadn't shattered in the windshield of her mother's hatchback before Vivie went through it. Don't text and drive, don't text and drive, don't text and drive.

Dust and debris floated everywhere. A poop-covered bird feather settled on Vivie's blood-soaked purple hair. If she were still alive, she would have been more upset about this than having wrecked her mother's car (therefore having no easy transportation until it was fixed or replaced). I couldn't believe the cell phone that had killed her was still in her hand until I recalled reading something back in the day about "the death clutch"—pretty much instant *rigor mortis* of a body part. Science-y stuff is so interesting, isn't it?

Her aura glowing with flashing shards of angry orange and immature pink, Vivie sat to the side with her mouth hanging open. Knowing what I do about surprise deaths, I was sure she would be sitting like this for years unless somebody came to collect her. Aside from her mother, who didn't believe in anything much anymore, there would be only a few sad friends depositing flowers, candles, cards and teddy bears at this soon-to-be briefly famous spot under the overpass for the next few days, thinking only of themselves and their own sorrow and not about what Vivie was about to experience in the weeks, maybe years to come.

I had to get her out of there before she expended all her energy and dissipated into nothing but a ghost, a big concern for us when one of our Charges bites it violently.

And by the way, despite what you might have heard, we refer to ourselves as Guides, not Guardian Angels. I once referred to myself as an angel in front of Pete and he laughed so hard he accidentally farted.

So. How was I going to handle this? I had been assigned to Vivie when she turned thirteen, a special age in many cultures. I wasn't much older than she was when Pete gave me the job. I think the only time she noticed I was there was when her bunny rabbit, Petunia, died. How long ago was that anyway? Time doesn't really concern us over here so I can't really pinpoint any kind of date. When Petunia was laid to rest in the flower garden in front of her mother's house, Vivie seemed to sense me but she thought I was Petunia.

Aha. That might work. I approached Vivie.

Two

Traffic had slowed in both directions of the four-lane. I heard someone in the near lane scream in horror from the passenger seat as a truck puttered past the carnage. I couldn't tell whether it had been a man, a woman—or a child—but the scream was echoed by distant sirens.

I needed to get Vivie away from there as quickly and as calmly as I could. There's nothing worse than a panicked Charge at the point of Transition. I approached her.

"Hi there. How are you?"

Could I have said anything lamer?

Let's try this again. "Hi there. My name's Petunia. What's yours?"

It seems I *could* say something lamer. I tried hard not to roll my eyes. If Vivie caught me doing that, she'd think the look was aimed at her.

She continued to ignore me, so I decided to forget the niceties. "I know your name is Vivie. We have to get out of here. Right now. No arguments." I grasped her elbow and boosted her to her feet. She offered no resistance. So far so good.

Elbows hooked, we headed up the rise alongside the cement pillar at the base of which lay her cooling body. At the top of the rise, a slight shimmer of the air parted revealing a stone tunnel. I pointed. "See the light at the far end?"

Vivie said nothing and gave no indication she had heard me.

"That's what we're aiming for," I said. "If for some unthinkable reason we become separated, that's where you have to go. Do you understand me? Vivie?" I could only hope I got through to her this time.

Behind us and down below, an ambulance, a fire truck, two police cars and a TV SUV pulled in, filling the area with red and blue lights—and authority. Beside me, Vivie shuddered and turned her head slowly around. I didn't want her to see anything. I needed to get her into the tunnel.

"Let's go, Vivikins." And I more or less pushed her into the tunnel. Now if only I could get her through it without her seeing anybody. Yeah, right.

Three

As we headed in, I let her walk along by herself.

I was nervous even though Guides are supposed to be stalwart and steadfast, but this was always the most difficult area to get through with our Charges. Hah. Listen to me, will you! "Stalwart and steadfast?" What was I, a Marine or something? I'm glad Pete wasn't around to hear me think that. I was even laughing at myself. Nerves are funny things, aren't they?

As we moved along the tunnel, I knew Vivie wasn't seeing it the way it was. Guides are often able to get into our Charges' heads and I could tell she was seeing a high school corridor in the morning, complete with lockers, gawkers, bullies, nerds and the untouchable elite. I didn't dare tell her she was seeing things. This was her least favorite part of the school day so, of course, she was going to picture something like this.

"Atta girl. Let's just move along, shall we." It wasn't a question, it was a gentle suggestion. Well, maybe a firm suggestion. I tried to grasp her elbow, but she jumped as though a spider web had just draped itself over her arm. All right, I'll try something else. I pointed toward the end of the long stone tunnel. "See that light down there? Way down there. It's barely visible as more than a flicker but it's there, you can trust me on that. Do you see it?"

I was happy she squinted her eyes toward it. Bonus! We were connecting. Was she finally hearing my voice? Would she continue to hear my voice? For her sake I hoped so.

To be perfectly honest with you, this tunnel isn't made of stone. I don't know what it's made of. I just know that it's solid and gray. I wouldn't call it cement, but I wouldn't call it pure stone either. It's a mishmash from the imagination of every single being who has ever passed through it. But I wasn't about to tell Vivie this. Not until I had to and only—hopefully—*if*.

It's true that there were people—young people—along the walls of the tunnel, and they were real, but most of them had no interest in us whatsoever. They were too busy thumbing their imaginary communication devices. Those who were watching us pass stared at us with a mixture of fear and longing, the tattered rags of their long-out-of-date clothing unnoticed to themselves.

Vivie became aware of my presence. She didn't actually turn to me. I think she'd realized finally, who—or should I say what—I was. Somebody living in her head? *How was this supposed to make her feel better*? I asked, hoping Pete would be listening in.

She spoke: "What are they all staring at?"

Trying to sound cheery and upbeat I responded with "Why, *you*, of course." This was true absolutely. Nobody could see *me*. Well, almost nobody.

"I don't like it. Not at all. Make them stop."

"How am I supposed to do that? I have no control over anything other than myself."

This time, she gave me The Look. "I get, like, these feelings about you. Like, you're the same age as me, but it feels like you're my mother or something. You're some kind of a boss around here. Make them stop."

"No can do, Vivikins. No can do."

"Now you're really creeping me out."

I raised my eyebrows in a question and tried to stop my grin. I knew exactly why.

"That's what my father always calls me. Vivikins."

"Yes, I know."

The Look again. "You seem to know an awful lot about me. Like I said, it's creepy. So stop it. And stop them from looking at me."

I leaned in as though to whisper a secret. "If you didn't want people looking at you, why did you color your hair purple?"

She rolled her eyes.

I laughed. "Seems you've heard that one before."

"A million times."

"A whole million, eh? Not nine hundred and ninety-nine thousand nine hundred and ninety-nine times?"

She stifled a laugh. "Don't be a smart butt."

I said it and I meant it: "It's always nice to see you laugh."

We were now passing a small group of girls around Vivie's age. There were four of them. Cheerleader types complete with pom-poms and cute little uniforms. In pink, if you can believe it.

"I'm guessing your favorite color is pink?"

She zoned out on me at that point because along came George and his goons.

Toad poop! This was the very person I was hoping to avoid. And what was he doing in this area? He was banned from here. Oh, ha. When did George ever obey the rules?

The cheerleaders erupted in a flurry of pink pom-poms and giggles as they chanted: "Georgie Porgie, puddin' and pie, kissed the girls and made them cry."

One of the goons came right up to Vivie and leaned into her space. "You're new here, aren't you? Love the hair."

Vivie cringed.

"C'mon. You gotta meet George. He's the coolest dude this side of The Veil." The goon snatched at Vivie's upper arm.

She jumped back and for a fraction of a second, disconnected with him mentally and turned slightly toward me. But George was in her face pushing his goon out of the way.

"I'll take over from here, Joey. Isn't she a delight? Hi there. I'm George." George bowed deeply without taking his eyes from Vivie's.

"Her name's Vivie," said one of the cheerleaders, stepping up to George and lacing her arm through his. "She's new here."

George raised one eyebrow and looked Vivie up and down. "So I understand." At that moment, his entire demeanor changed and he performed a pirouette coming out of it fully adorned in a suit of armor complete with sword and shield.

Although I tried to stop it, my eyes rolled up into my head and I said "toad poop" out loud. Vivie had just finished reading an article about Saint George and the Dragon. *Ack.*

Joey and the other goons laughed as George looked down at himself.

"Hey, I like this. Whaddaya think, boys? Pretty snappy, isn't it?" Then his eyes bore into Vivie's again. "I believe this little gal's a keeper."

Vivie shivered.

The cheerleader who had been on George's arm stepped between him and Vivie, her back to Vivie. "C'mon, honey. Let's get out of here."

George pushed her away. "Mind your own business, Linda. You're always interfering with everything."

Vivie was so enamored with George's transition, she missed this action. "Are you, like, *Saint* George? The guy who killed the dragon? I read about him. Er, you."

Joey and the goons and the cheerleaders—even Linda— burst into laughter.

When Joey had collected himself and had wiped the wetness from his eyes, he said, "No, sweetie, this dude is the dragon itself."

Another burst of laughter erupted from everyone but George who, behind Joey, and no longer in his suit of armor, grabbed Joey by the shirt collar and roughly dragged him backwards. He threw him onto the tunnel floor. "I told you before don't mock me. You know what happens to people who mock me."

Joey scrambled to where the other goons stood. The cheerleaders huddled together except for Linda who came forward.

"Take it easy, honey," she said, rubbing one of George's shoulder blades. "He didn't mean nothing by that." This was the first time I noticed that Linda's hair was done up like Joan Crawford's in all those old 1940's and 1950's film noir movies I loved so much when I was on the Earth Plane. I guess they weren't all *that* old when I was on the Earth Plane. In the late 1950s and early 1960s, I was old enough to stay up on weekends, so I watched late movies on television and that's when and why I fell in love with them. And our new friend, Linda, on closer examination, was older than I had originally thought.

"Let's go." George shrugged Linda off. "I've had enough of this snooty witch." He sneered at Vivie then turned on his heel and disappeared into an opening in the tunnel wall. Without protest or comment of any kind, his goons and the cheerleaders followed.

I didn't have to wonder where that had come from. George's viewpoints and moods swung like the pendulum in the 1961 movie, *The Pit and the Pendulum*, the last movie I ever saw at the drive-in. Come to think of it, heading home with my boyfriend in his parents' car that night was the last thing I ever *did* on the Earth Plane. I have no idea what happened as I was distracted, desperately wanting to make notes. The movie had inspired me with half a dozen good story ideas.

Vivie "wanted to be a writer," too. That's why I got assigned to her. She wasn't exactly texting per se, she was making notes. She "couldn't possibly" lose THAT train of thought, THAT marvelous idea. Oh, how I understood that passion! But… *Don't text and drive, Vivie! Don't text and drive.* She hadn't heard me, and it was my fault.

And now, here we were together on this side of The Veil. Karma maybe? It was a rough enough assignment following around a young writer on the Earth Plane. *Here*, things could change—*SNAP!*—in a thought-space. This was going to be, to misquote Bette Davis, one bumpy ride.

Four

<u>Section One</u>

I DON'T KNOW HOW I did it, but I managed to get Vivie to the Community Center area in one piece. As we stepped from tunnel to turf into Section One, though, something drew my attention off to the side where a hitherto empty meadow now contained a saloon, a dirt street, wooden sidewalks, a sheriff's office and a general store right out of an old Saturday afternoon matinee cowboy movie from my day. Yep, I was around Vivie's age, but I was older than dirt.

I tried my best to hustle her past this unexpected apparition without success because just then, and just like in the movies, a cowboy, hat and all, came flying through the saloon's swinging doors and landed face down in the dirt. At the doors, a burly guy in an apron wiped his hands together and shouted: "And stay out until your head clears, Hiram."

Vivie, always the kind-hearted soul, rushed over to offer help.

By the time she got to him, he was on his feet, brushing himself off.

Now keep in mind that Vivie was wearing a cute little tank top with Grumpy Cat on the front, her bra straps showing at the shoulders; distressed jeans with her knees sticking out; and mile-high shoes with gladiator straps nearly up to her kneecaps. And don't forget the purple hair. Although this cowboy was not within my purview, I took great pride in the look on his face when he spotted Vivie. This man might never, ever, touch another glass of whiskey. He took off.

I was now close enough to Vivie to see the absolute desolation on her face. I don't blame her. If someone had looked at me as though I were a thing from another planet—and I mean *The* Thing as in the movie of the same name—I would have been devastated, too. At that point she turned to me and I think she saw me as I am. The tears welling from her eyes made me want to hold her as though she were a toddler who had just had the fright of his life. But events were so strange to her at this moment, touching her would have sent her screaming into the hills. Or worse, a complete shut-down.

"This way," I said, and I encouraged her into the meadow of flowers that lay between us and the vast Community-Center-plus that sat with its back against the forest.

Once again, she mentally drifted away from me but, to my relief, she continued toward the Community Center anyway. As we reached the Center's main building, I wondered how she would react to what was inside and behind it and vice versa: how people would react to her. Although I knew folks were used to all manner of newcomers showing up at all hours and wearing clothing from every period in history, purple hair was something relatively new here. So were those mile-high shoes. And what was behind that door was nothing like Vivie had ever seen except, perhaps, in her writerly imagination.

Just as her foot touched the bottom step of the Center's porch at the main door, a clatter of horse and wagon made both of us turn around.

It was Hiram leading a Hoe & Shovel Mob, a standard in western movies. If Vivie and I ever got to actual talking, that was going to be the second thing I asked her about. Maybe even the first thing: *What's with all the 1950's movies in your head? Have I influenced you that much?*

"There she is!" cried one of the men brandishing a hoe as he jumped from the wagon, nearly putting out the eye of the man behind him. "String 'er up."

A mutter of agreement flowed through the men as they collected themselves in a cluster behind Hiram, one of them actually working a rope into the thirteen knots officially required for a noose.

The murmuring continued as Hiram, like a birthday party clown, dragged a handkerchief the size of a table runner out of a back pocket and sopped the moisture off his forehead. He returned the handkerchief to its pocket before stepping forward, his other thick-fingered hand twisting around a scythe.

"If you come along peacefully, young lady, it'll go easier for you."

Behind us, the door to the main entrance of the Community Center banged open to disgorge my friend Maria and her Charge, Eduardo, one of the most handsome young men I'd ever had the pleasure to lay my eyes on both here and on the Earth Plane. Down the steps of the porch they came.

"Hey, 'Petunia,'" teased Maria, "what's going on? Your Charge giving you grief, too?"

"A tad." With my chin I indicated Hiram's lynch mob. "They've never seen anything like her before."

"Neither have I," she laughed. Maria was always laughing. Not in a mean way although it felt like that sometimes. "Want me to get Eduardo here involved? Might take his mind off a certain issue he's dealing with. Again."

"That would be beyond peachy if you were to do that. And soon."

By this time, four men had surrounded Vivie and were

attempting to tie her wrists together with thin rope—I think it's called binder twine—without a lot of success. I had to give it to her, she was feisty. *That's my girl!*

Eduardo stepped up. "Excuse me. What do you think you are doing? Leave this young lady be."

Although Eduardo wasn't much older than Vivie, he had an air of authority about him that could not be denied. Like drops of mercury from a broken thermometer, the mob rippled away from Vivie and from each other. Hoe Man urged his buddies back onto the wagon and off they went in the clichéd cloud of dust.

Eduardo stepped in to undo the twine that bound Vivie's wrists. "If you massage that, it will prevent bruising."

Vivie said nothing but looked up at Eduardo with awe. Can't say I blamed her.

"You are new here." If Eduardo had looked at me the way he was looking at Vivie right then I would have fainted. "Come with me." He offered his arm.

Back on the porch now and holding the Community Center door open, Maria hollered to the interior. "Newbie coming. Clear the decks!"

Stunned to silence, one arm hooked through the sideways V of his elbow, and obediently massaging a wrist, Vivie floated along beside Eduardo. I followed her, but as I passed Maria, Maria whispered, "We haven't heard the last of that bunch I'm afraid."

I nodded worried agreement.

"But what's with the western movie theme and your girl anyway? Have you been hiding her somewhere for the last sixty years?" Tossing her head back, Maria let loose a hearty guffaw.

Five

Eduardo was kind enough to take Vivie on a tour of what was actually a small village attached to the main building—he was like that with everyone: kind—but I don't know how much she absorbed. I think she was still recovering from almost being lynched by her own imagination coupled, no doubt, with mine. But that would be a good thing, it meant we had connected closely after all.

While Eduardo and Vivie chatted small talk about the never-closed bar with its 24/7 music blasting out of it; the convenience store with its full array of chemicals, depressants and addictives in the guise of bags of chips, cookies and cigarettes; the restaurant that offered everything from every cuisine on Earth; and the several other stores—each establishment with names so cutesy it almost made my brain cramp—Maria and I did a bit of catch-up.

"So, *Petunia*," she said in that special way that always made me brace myself against what would be coming out of her mouth next. "What have *you* been up to lately? We haven't seen you for *ages*."

She was using the royal we now? Humility was not Maria's forte. This could be for one of two reasons: her Charges passed through to the next level quickly because of her competence; or she was lousy at her job, so they assigned the easiest Charges to her. Eduardo seemed to me to be an easy one but obviously, since he had been here in Section One for such a long time—years, in fact—maybe there was something I wasn't seeing. Maria had managed to get him out once, but here he was back again.

"Ya just gotta love that name! *Petunia.*" A laugh erupted. "Of all the names you could have chosen, you picked *Petunia.*" She poked me with her elbow. "Ha ha. Freudian slip there. *Picked* Petunia? Get it?" And on she guffawed.

"Hey. Shut up for a minute."

"I see no cause for rudeness, Susan!" she snapped, using my real name.

Before she could continue, I snapped back, "Where did they go? I thought you had him under control. You've certainly had enough time to work on him."

She opened her mouth to say something, but I refused to listen to another word.

"No, no. There's no need to apologize to *me*. Of course not." I took off to where I had last seen them. Toad poop. "You made me lose track of my Charge! Yours, too, by the looks of it."

"What?"

"They took off."

"No way," she said, not laughing now. "I thought you were messing with my head. Like, *joking*, y'know?"

I could hear her feet slapping the ground behind me as I ran.

I knew before I rounded the corner of the convenience store into the tunnel-like alley between it and the hospital, that Vivie and Eduardo had encountered something unpleasant. Some*body* unpleasant. And there he was in all his glory: George, complete with Linda on his arm, and his goons and the other three cheerleaders watching from the sidelines.

There would be no scaring-off of this crew like Eduardo had managed with Hiram's mob. Nope. In fact, Eduardo was standing slightly behind Vivie, his eyes even more wide and fear-filled than hers. George and Vivie were already in mid-conversation.

As Maria and I approached the group, I knew that Vivie had become aware of my presence. It looked like the same thing had happened for Eduardo and Maria. Good.

George was grinning into Vivie's face. "A simple party. Everybody loves the parties I throw." He turned to his goons and the cheerleaders. "Isn't that right, ladies and germs?" He waved his hands toward himself to elicit a suitable response to his question.

The goons and the cheerleaders mumbled a unanimous "Ahum."

"That settles it then." He tossed a big ol' smile at Vivie, then turned to Linda. "What's her name again?"

"Vivie."

"That's right. Vivie. Vivie will be attending our party." He glommed onto Vivie's hand. I think she was too scared to protest. "And the show starts when? Come on everybody. The show starts when?" George's minions uttered a very unenthusiastic "now" compared with his ear-splitting *"NOW! Let's get this show on the road, baby."*

Vivie shot a glance back to her Eduardo but received only a helpless shrug from him. The glance I shot at Eduardo's Guide, Maria, elicited a shrug from her as well, albeit, hers was accompanied by a face full of pleading horror.

Before I could react, George had spirited Vivie and his minions right through the wall of the tunnel.

"No, no, no, no, no! Oh, Vivie," I yelled after her. "If you've never listened to me before, please do it now." My hands formed a cone in front of my mouth. "Do not listen to one single word

George tells you." I tucked my love beads inside the collar of my tie-dyed T-shirt (both, gifts from Maria because, she said, I had missed "the *best* era in *all* of history") and set off behind the group. "Toad poop and toad pee, too. Oh man."

Six

WHEN I GOT TO THE spot where George had disappeared with Vivie, I realized they had gone through an imaginary doorway. I felt Eduardo behind me and turned to him. Without thinking, I asked him "Where did they go?"

"Duh," said Maria. "He can't hear you." She turned to Eduardo, "Yo, sugar-pie. Where did they go?"

"You talk to him like that?"

"Why not? He doesn't exactly hear my words, just the concept. Right?"

"Ask him again."

She did.

Eduardo took off running along the alley.

Maria, always the smart butt, put two fingers of each hand against her temples and closed her eyes. Raising her face upward, she said, "I sense there's a doorway farther down the tunnel. I sense that my Charge knows about this."

"This is not the least bit funny." I took off as fast as I could, calling back, "When this gets done, you, my dear Maria, are going to get one resounding kick where you sit."

Ahead of her once again, I heard Maria's breathless voice, "Don't make me laugh."

Up ahead, Eduardo disappeared through what I remembered was a gate that had been there for probably forever. With Maria on my heels, I ducked through the gate to find myself in what looked and felt like an airplane cockpit with its one-hundred-and-eighty-degree-plus window on the world. And there was Vivie, her back to me, George's arm draped over it, as she stared down into some kind of religious building where a service was going on. George's goons and the cheerleaders surrounded them, making it impossible for Eduardo to get close enough to pull Vivie out of their midst, so he fidgeted from foot to foot behind the group.

Maria leaned into my space and asked if I were OK.

"Why?"

"You gasped so loudly I thought you were having an asthma attack. You sure you're OK?"

"That—" Oh, I could think of a word for George, but I wasn't about to say it. I was not about to either mess up the color of my aura or diminish its energy level because of the likes of him. I pushed the word and my feelings toward him from my mind.

Maria leaned in and patted my shoulder. "I know. I know. He did the same thing to Eduardo when he first got here." She made eye contact with me. "I got Eduardo away, but it didn't take George long to hunt him down."

"I know being this close to Section Two isn't a good place for your Charge, either. Maybe if Vivie were out of his sphere of influence—"

"You and your big words."

I continued. "Maybe if Vivie were out of Eduardo's sphere of influence, she might hear me."

"I know. I know." Maria patted my shoulder again.

"And he would hear you better, too? To get him out of here to where he's supposed to be?"

Maria stepped ahead of me. "I'll see what I can do."

"Thanks, eh?"

"That's OK. You can owe me one. Another one." Maria moved up to stand directly behind Eduardo. She looked back at me. "Wish me luck."

"You know as well as I do that it takes a lot more than luck in this place."

After a thumb's up to me she leaned forward to whisper into Eduardo's ear.

As though a brilliant idea had just flashed through his head, Eduardo brightened, turned and fled past me back the way we had come. On her hurried way by, I got two thumbs up from Maria.

I was several feet away from Vivie, but her voice was loud and clear: "They're all so sad! Why are they crying? This is awful. That's Mom. That's my brother Zach. And Dad? What's Dad doing there? Mom and Dad are divorced. And some of the guys from my school are there."

As George's hand caressed Vivie's back, Linda moved to the other side of her and leaned in to say, "Same thing happened to me. It was awful. My parents divorced too, and I know it was all my fault."

Across the top of Vivie's head, George smiled at Linda who did not return his smile. In fact, I thought I saw a glint of a tear in Linda's eye before she turned her face away.

I was now close enough to Vivie to see the frown pinch her face. "How could it be your fault? Or mine? That's stupid. Dad told me it wasn't anything to do with anything. These things happen. When you're young, you're foolish, he told me. He and Mom were only eighteen when they got married."

George snickered. "And, of course, you believed him. Him being your dad and all. You probably thought your parents were perfect. Right?"

"There's nothing wrong with my parents. Look at them." Vivie pointed through the window of the airplane's cockpit at the scenario unfolding below. "They're even holding hands."

After a quick upturn of George's chin in her direction, Linda sighed then spoke again to Vivie. Linda would never win an Academy Award for acting, but her sneer was effective. "You don't get it, do you? It's all your fault they got divorced and even if they didn't get a divorce before, they would now anyway. Don't you know that when something bad happens to a child the family falls apart? Especially when it's the child's fault?"

"Something bad happened? You mean to me? I… I… What do you mean?" Vivie looked down at herself. "What's going on? I don't like it. Make it stop. What did I do?" She tried to struggle away from George and Linda to get closer to the window, but they were holding her back with practiced hands and arms. "Mommy. Daddy. I'm so sorry. Zach, I'm sorry. I didn't mean to do anything bad."

Oh, I didn't like where this was going. I expected it from George, and somewhat from Linda, the 1940's bad girl, but I didn't think Vivie would be this easily convinced to go on a guilt trip, the last thing anybody this close to Section Two should ever even *think* about doing. When I was in high school, and because I "wanted to be a writer," I loved *Macbeth*, especially the scene where he comes across the witches who pretty much let him know what's going to happen to him, so this jumped into my head:

Double, double toil and trouble;
Fire burn and cauldron bubble.

Vivie had to learn, and quickly, the lesson: just because somebody you think might be in-the-know says you're heading in a certain direction or that you belong in a place or must remain in a situation, it doesn't mean you're stuck with it. But that doesn't mean it's going to be easy getting out of it, either.

The window of the airplane's cockpit disappeared, and George and Linda led Vivie off—a lot more gently than I would have imagined. But "candy" doesn't always come out of a box or wrapped in little bits of waxed paper, does it?

Seven

<u>Section Two</u>

"WHY ARE YOU GOING TO all this trouble for me?"

"What do you mean?" said George, eyes darting back and forth. "Why wouldn't I? You're a sweet gal."

Seriously? He was going to pull that old line on my Charge?

Regardless, I had work to do. And I could only hope that Maria was having a good talking-to with her Charge, Eduardo. I was thinking that Eduardo was our only hope but not the way everything was at this stage. He would be in grave danger if he returned to Section Two. He could jeopardize not only himself, but Vivie, Maria, and me.

I knew from the training I got from Pete that George's goal was to get as many newcomers into Section Two as he could. When I was in little-kid school on the Earth Plane, we were taught about armies of angels. Good angels and bad angels. It certainly scared the "Hell" out of me, and that's no joke. Things changed for me, though, when I myself became an "angel"—sorry, Pete. Being on this side of The Veil and especially working here, wasn't anything like we were taught or what I expected. What some very lucky people were taught and accepted back on the Earth Plane was that life is what you make it. That was no truer on Earth than it was here. In fact, it was truer here. That's what was frightening me the most. George had an amazing talent for talking people into believing him and believing *in* him, too. No doubt about that. He must have been a politician in a former life, ha ha, not funny. Perhaps George didn't want anyone to advance further than this section because *he* couldn't? I had no idea why he might not be able to go further, that was between him and his Guide. If he even still had one. I know if I had been his Guide, I would be hanging my head in shame in some dark, dank cellar corner right about now as far away from him as I could get and not caring if I dissipated. But it wasn't up to me to do any judging of anyone. I wasn't perfect. Nobody around here was.

Main thing was, I had to stop what he was going to be doing to *my* Charge, Vivie. She was my responsibility and we Guides take our responsibilities way more seriously than anyone can believe. And not simply for altruistic reasons either. Like I said, if we didn't do our job properly, we would be in big trouble, too. Maybe that's what had happened with George. Had he been stuck with Linda, the bad girl from the 1940s as his Charge? If so, that wasn't fair. She was no worse than I. Except I had already been promoted to Guide and she was still moving back and forth from Section One to Section Two with George siphoning energy from her whenever he wanted to. If I could get her away from him, she might be able to help me with Vivie. If she still had enough energy to sustain both herself and George, there still had to be kindness inside her. If Maria couldn't get Eduardo ready and strong enough, Linda might be Vivie's last chance. I didn't trust Linda though. I would have to hope that Maria was coming along well with Eduardo, so he could help with Vivie. Maria had absolutely no responsibility toward my Charge, but Maria and I went way back and, like she said, I owed her a few favors, and she owed me favors, too. That's another thing we all did here, we tried our best to get our guys together to help each other not only on the Earth Plane but here, too, once our Charges arrived.

Oh, George, George, George. Was he doing all this using-of-others toward his own ends, to prevent himself from dissipating? How long had he been here? Neither Maria nor I had ever been able to figure out what historical era George had come from. It could have been millennia ago or decades ago because no matter what you said to him, or asked him, he had an answer. No matter what, we had to stop him. Both Maria and I knew that Eduardo would want to help with Vivie's rescue, but he would be greatly endangered if he tried. We could not risk losing either of them, let alone both. Nor could we risk ourselves because they'd be in even more dire straits without us.

Did I dare leave Vivie alone with George and his minions while I went to consult with Pete, I mean Trevor?

I had no choice.

Eight

<u>Community Center</u>

I MANAGED TO LOCATE MARIA as soon as I entered the Center. She and Eduardo were standing on the sidewalk, Eduardo staring down at a small bottle of what looked like brandy in his hand. Hey, no light beer for this boy. I now understood Maria's predicament concerning Eduardo. He had problems with accepting his limitations—such as they might be. It happens with good people who aren't always able to do what their dreams entice them to do. Instead of trying harder, failing, yet trying again and again in different ways until they at last succeed, they reach for oblivion instead and think of themselves as weak and useless which is usually as far from the truth as it can get, but it proves their point.

"Sorry to interrupt, Maria—"

Startled, she jumped. "Yikes. You could warn a girl, y'know."

"I have to consult with a certain somebody. And right now."

"With who?"

"With whom."

"SUSAN! Don't do this."

"Sorry. Stress brings out my internal editor. Where is he?"

"He? Tell me you're not talking about *Trevor*?" Maria threw her arms into the air in frustration. "What do you want Saint Pete for?"

"Don't ask."

"OK I won't ask. I think maybe I don't *want* to know? Is that *close*?"

I could only nod my head.

"Oh, Susie. Oh, my dear Susie-Q. George got her away from you. What*ever* are you going to *do*?"

"I have no choice. I have to go begging."

"I wouldn't want to be in your shoes right about now. Vivie's either for that matter." Maria's eyes met mine and I had never seen such genuine concern in them. This didn't make me feel any better.

"So… Do you know where he is? Is he still around?"

Maria pointed in the direction of the mall. "Oh, he's still around all right. Who do you think talked my boy here into the brandy?"

"Is he still in the liquor store?"

Maria's laugh was a cross between a Linda-like sneer—but an authentic one—and a snarl. "You know he kinda likes to move around."

"*MARIA!*"

"Last I saw of him he was in the fast food place urging Lizzie toward a third helping of fries."

I headed for Patates at as dead a run as I could manage.

Behind me, Maria called out, "With gravy and grits. And cheese. You don't always have to shoot yourself in the head to commit suicide."

I knew that.

I also knew what was going on "back at the ranch," as they say. Vivie was freaking out. I could feel it. I had to find Trevor a.k.a. Pete, get some quick advice from him, try to convince him to maybe even pitch in, then get back to Vivie sooner than soonest.

I found him at Patates. And yes, he was urging poor sweet Lizzie, all poor sweet six hundred pounds of her to *"Mangia! Mangia!* Go ahead. Live your dream. Get it out of your system." Then: "Whatever you do, don't try to find out what food is a substitute for."

"Hey, Lizzie," I said. I knew she couldn't hear me, but I had to say it anyway. "I trust that all is well with you?"

"Hey, yourself," Trevor spouted from his big fake smile. "Nice to see you. Long time, huh? Uh, Sandra, right?"

"Uh, yeah. Sure. Sandra. Close enough. I need your help, Trevor."

"Ah. So *now* she needs me."

"I do. My Charge is recently arrived. Quickly and violently."

"Suicide?"

I shook my head. "Texting and driving."

Trevor shrugged. "Same thing pretty much. What's happening?"

"One word. George."

Trevor snapped his head to one side and grimaced. "Oh, dear. OK. You get back to your Charge and I'll see what I can do from here. Expect help from someone interesting." His grin was now genuine but annoying as I had seen that grin before and knew what it portended. He would make a good choice for my teammate/mentor, but Trevor believed that everybody had to do everything the hard way.

As I was turning away, someone I'd never met came running up to Trevor, and this guy was as out of breath as anyone could be. "Oh no, oh no, oh no. We need everybody we can get. We have a sudden influx coming in at Section Three." The guy caught his breath. "Oodles. They haven't hit yet." Another deep breath. "But it's imminent. Please. Get help to Section Three."

"No problem, my boy. I'll head to Control Central immediately." To Lizzie he said. "Listen sweetheart, I have to go now. We got a big emergency coming in as we speak. You're just going to have to handle things the best you can by yourself for now. OK? You're going to be aaaalll alone for a loooong time. Nobody loves you."

Trevor a.k.a. Pete turned to me then and shrugged broadly, hands in the air. "It's the only way to make her listen to me. She won't take advice dispensed in any other manner. Stubborn girl."

Much as I hated to admit it, Trevor knew what he was doing. Especially in an emergency situation. I couldn't help myself, I said, "Finally going to be doing something at the level of your pay grade for a change, huh?"

"Laugh all you want but it's an all-hands-on-deck thing right now. This means we are going to be using you, too." He looked at me with his silly grin. I couldn't tell if he was joking or not. Something told me he wasn't. "Yes. You. We're that desperate. Let's go, kiddo. Off with you now. But go to Section Two first. That's where your girl is."

I beat feet for Section Two.

Nine

<u>Section Two</u>

WHEN I WAS ON THE Earth Plane, my mother would sometimes accuse me of exaggerating. I preferred the word "embellish" myself, and told her so, often. Mom was a straight shooter about pretty much everything. A tree was a tree to her, where I, the wannabe writer, would say something more along the lines of "the lonely oak on yonder hill, bony arms raised in supplication to the heavens." OK, OK. But it's not a lie. Right?

What I'm about to tell you is no embellishment, no exaggeration, no lies. It really happened. All of it. (Although I still have trouble believing most of it.) Maybe that's whom I am trying to convince. *Moi.*

By the time I got back to Section Two, Vivie and George were playing tug-of-war with a bewildered little bald girl around the age of seven or eight, wearing a hospital gown, and clutching a teddy bear dressed up as a doctor. She had huge gray splotches below her eyes and was even trailing an IV tube from her skinny left arm. Not hard to guess where she had transitioned from: a children's hospital.

"Let her go," demanded Vivie.

"I can't," George snapped at her. "She's valuable."

He motioned for Linda to step in and she did. Immediately.

But not with her normal enthusiasm. "Georgie…" she whined, pushing Vivie aside. "She's not much more than a baby. Look at her. Imagine what she's been through. Don't do this, Georgie."

"Shut up, Linda. Can't you hear it? Can't you hear its mother's voice screaming in sorrow over the loss of her daughter? Screaming *loudly*? A little *too* loudly? Asking that this precious child stay forever close to her?"

Linda shrugged and shook her head. "You're right. Mommy's grief doesn't sound all that sincere to me."

George grasped the little bald girl by the shoulders and turned her to face Linda. "This lamb chop ain't going nowheres for a long time. She'll be sticking around to please Mommy." He leaned down to speak to the side of the little bald girl's face. "Right Lamb Chop? Mommy wants you to stick around, doesn't she?" Then again to Linda, and with his eyes taking Vivie in, too, he said, "I might as well take advantage of the situation. Can't pass up on fresh young energy, can I?"

I now understood what this wee gal was doing in Section Two. Kids from hospitals were pretty much always well-versed on what was going to happen when they passed over, so they landed in a *named* section, not a numbered one. By the way, the higher the number in the numbered sections, the worse things are there.

Trevor a.k.a. Pete had stuck the name "Blissland" on the section Little Bald Girl should have shot to instantly, because, according to him, that's what those people felt when the pain abruptly went away never to come back: pure bliss. But "Blissland" wasn't anywhere near here so Little Bald Girl had been misdirected. Perhaps by a greedy mother? You see, it's rare, but there are women, occasionally men, who make their own children ill—even poison them—so *they* can get attention. That's what must have happened here. I could only hope Little Bald Girl's Guide would be able to work with that.

Speaking of whom… a Guide with a black eye and several snapped-off and bent wing feathers staggered onto the scene.

"Ah, there you are," he managed to say to Little Bald Girl while bending down to grasp his knees and breathing hard. "I was looking for you in Blissland. Then elsewhere." He stretched out one of his hands, palm up, to her. "But we won't go into detail about that right now. Maybe not ever." With that hand, he then pushed away a bent wing feather that was threatening to poke Little Bald Girl in the face. He held his hand out to her again. "Let's go."

"Wings, Dougie?" I said, grinning despite the seriousness of the situation. "That is so… so… so *passé*."

"More like *de rigueur*," Dougie said, brushing himself off. "You have to go with what they'll accept."

I knew that.

A combination shiver-shake sent his damaged wings flying into perfection again, but the black eye remained. He repeated his request to Little Bald Girl. She made no sign of having heard or seen him. She seemed to be far away somewhere. Her teddy bear dangled from her left hand, the IV tubing in that arm swinging back and forth across its face.

George though, George saw and heard him. "She's staying here."

At this, Linda shook her head and stepped away. Maybe there was hope for "Joan Crawford."

"*That* one, though," he said, jabbing a finger in Vivie's direction, "Take her instead of this one." He pulled Little Bald Girl closer to himself. "You can leave right now and take that one with you." To Linda he said, "Her name's Vivie, right?"

Linda did not respond.

"Yeah." George's eyes squinted into unreadable slits at Linda before he widened them at Dougie. "Her name's Vivie. You can take *Vivie* and drop her off in Section Three on your way by and don't let the door hit your rear end on the way out, *Dougie*."

Dougie stepped up so close to George's face, their noses touched. "*NO!*"

George stepped back. He swatted his fingers against his nose before yelling out, without turning around: "Joey. You take her then. Off this defiant witch goes to Section Three." He rubbed at his nose again.

Linda shook her head so vehemently a bobby pin went flying. "No, no, Georgie. Vivie's a good kid, she doesn't belong there. Her death was violent, yes, but not *that* violent."

George shot something between a pout and a sneer at Linda. "And good riddance. I don't know what I was thinking wanting to keep the likes of her around." He glared at me, then. "Writers! I should have known better." George's grin was cruel. Still holding Little Bald Girl who was making no move to get away from him—she was obviously used to obeying orders from not-so-nice adults—he now spun around to Joey and the other three goons. "Linda goes too."

I think I gasped along with everybody else when he said that.

Joey stepped forward. "You sure about that, boss?"

"Would I tell you to do it if I wasn't? Take her."

Joey shrugged as he turned to his fellow goons. "Well, I guess we have no choice, eh boys?"

Joey and the goons shuffled in to surround Linda.

George wiggled an index finger at the remaining cheer-leaders. "I'm sure you gals can handle this one on your own." Then his thumb pointed to Vivie. "Off yooze go."

I stepped forward at this point. "Whoa there!" I said to him, watching the cheerleaders lead Vivie off from the corner of my eye. "You can't do that. To put somebody in that section you either have to have permission or—"

Still holding Little Bald Girl under his arm, he twirled on

me. "I can do anything I bloody well please to do in this section—and in that one, too, I'll have you know."

I didn't know.

"Now be off with you, too." He flapped his free hand at me. "Do your job. Follow your Charge. Take good care of her." He laughed. "Better than you've been doing, at least. You guys always think you're so superior to the rest of us, don't you?" He raised the corner of his lip. "And look at you now."

I stepped to George and got up on my tiptoes. I couldn't exactly tower over him like Dougie had done—I wasn't anywhere near tall enough to do that, but I could at least pretend I was. Like Dougie had done, my eyes bore into George's, but there was no way I was going to touch noses with him. Just the thought of his touch was enough to make my aura fade. "Let that kid go and bring Vivie back here." With my eyes still on George's, I called out after Joey and the goons and the cheerleaders, "Joey! Linda! You guys don't have to listen to him." I wanted to blink but made myself control that urge. "When are you ever going to catch on to that?"

I knew they heard, but chose to ignore me. I broke eye contact with George and ran to catch up before they passed into Section Three, leaving Little Bald Girl and her Guide to work things out with George.

Behind me, Dougie hollered: "Thanks for trying. Break a wing, eh?"

I reached the end of the corridor at the exact same time Joey put his hand on the big steel door to Section Three and pushed. A gust of wind as strong as a black hole sucked us all into a huge, smelly cavern.

Ten

<u>Section Three</u>

BEFORE I COULD GET MY bearings in this cave that smelled somewhere between day-old roadkill and a high-school gym, a tremendous commotion erupted. I'm not exaggerating, I am truly not. An explosion of humanity came tumbling into the cave from somewhere above and to the side of us, all but two of them screaming, whether from fear or pain or both I couldn't tell yet. The messenger who had come running up to Trevor to warn him about this had not exaggerated either.

A quick count told me: four teenaged males, six teenaged females—no, wait, make that five teenaged females and one young adult female—two adult males, and a second adult female. A guy around seventeen years old, with the weirdest hairdo I'd ever seen, rolled in too. His hair was plastered flat on one side and on the other side it stuck straight out from his temple as though a bullet had just gone through. Or, wait a minute, maybe that's what had happened to him. Self-inflicted? Everybody else was yelling blue murder so loudly I wanted to cover my ears but didn't because I wanted to know what they were saying.

"RUN! RUN! RUN FOR YOUR LIVES!"

All four adults were attempting to herd the teenagers somewhere. I could see they were bewildered, not recognizing where they were.

Then in came thirteen Guides scrambling to meet up with their Charges. Absolute mayhem.

Weird Hair didn't seem to notice he was somewhere other than where he had expected to be as he was holding his head with both hands and moaning in great agony. So great was his pain, it seemed, all he could do was toddle in a tight circle like a little kid who had just dirtied his diaper. And I think he might have done just that. Normal instinct would have had me at his side instantly, to comfort him in his confusion and pain, but I felt nothing toward him. No compassion, no sense of anything being present inside him to draw me.

Beyond this madhouse of newcomers, Joey's group, with the protesting Linda in their midst, and the blank-faced cheer-leaders prodding a compliant Vivie, receded into the shadows at the far end of Section Three. *Please stay close till I finish up here. Please.*

I did a recount of Guides and newcomers and found I was short one Guide. Ah, there she was, sauntering in, working on the latest-model cell phone.

"Excuse me," I called out to her, not trying to hide my amazement at her nonchalance. "Does this dude belong to you?" I pointed at Weird Hair. "Aren't you supposed to be looking after him?"

"Huh?" She briefly glanced at me with bleary, bloodshot eyes. "Oh, him? Yeah. More or less." She resumed her thumbing.

"Aren't you going to help him?"

She didn't look up from her cell phone's screen. "*Argh,* missed it. Oh, yes, uh, you think he would have been reduced to this if he'd let me help him? *Ack,* missed it again. I did my best. I truly did."

"Oh no. You got stuck with one of those?"

"Indeed, I did." She removed her concentration from her cell phone and tucked it away into a pocket. She then made full-on eye contact with me and I knew then that those bleary, bloodshot eyes did not come from playing on a cell phone, they were from years of frustrated crying.

"OK if I hug you?" I asked.

She didn't say no so I did and I held her through several long moments of her body-shaking sobs of relief. Her job was done. This Charge would dissipate into nothing in no time.

Behind me, a loud *Ahem* turned me around to face Trevor a.k.a. Pete whose arms were folded and whose foot was tapping like Thumper's in that old Disney movie.

"Yes, boss. To the problem at hand I go." And I darted away to help with the newcomers.

****

This was my first mass entry so I was mostly all flailing fingers and dancing on tippy-toes until I figured out what was to be done. We needed to get everyone heading toward the Blissland area as soon as possible. Away from here as a first step, then along the safest route from there. It would not be an easy journey for them or for their Guides, two of whom I recognized, so I knew experience would be available if—let's change that to when—required.

As I began to follow along with the group of teens, adults, and their Guides, another loud *Ahem* behind me stopped me in my tracks. I didn't turn around because I didn't want Trevor to see the look on my face. Rather pointless, as he could see the frustrated, fearful orange shards in my aura. There were no secrets between Trevor and me.

"What?"

"Aren't you forgetting something, Sandra?"

"Susan. What? You told me to come here and help out." I

turned to face him.

"Yes. And you did. What's missing?"

"Nothing. She's right over—Oh! Where did she go? Toad poop!"

"Toad poop is right, Sandra. Last I saw of her she was with Linda's girls. Heading for Section Four."

<u>Section Four</u>

I pressed my way through the heavy iron entrance gate to Section Four. Nothing but a vast expanse of huge, empty, odorless soundlessness that went as far as the eye could see. No Joey, no goons, no Linda, no cheerleaders, no Vivie. Oh, wow. Where were they?

Then I saw something move over to one side. It looked like a round hay bale made of white feathers. The hay bale unfolded and became an old woman, white haired and dressed in a huge flowing white gown. Anything feathery about her fluttered away from the tips of her long arms and disappeared as she rose to her feet.

"Dirty old bean bags and rat rears, where am I?" She brushed herself off as she glanced around. "I'm gonna kill him. I'm gonna kill him."

I don't know how I knew but I did. She was talking about Trevor a.k.a. Pete.

I said "old" but because I was young, in my teens, she could have been anywhere between forty and ninety. Her vibe said one thing, but her face said another. Meaning her face was young and beautiful but, from some angles, she looked like the High Lama in the *Lost Horizons* movie. If I didn't know better, Trevor had come through and this was my new Guide.

In a huff, she stomped toward me. "You must be Sandra."

"Susan, actually."

"Whatever. Where did she go?"

I pasted on as sincere a smile as I could muster. "Who?" Um, no. Acting all innocent was not going to work with this babe. No way.

The old lady said nothing, and this made the deadly silence in this section even creepier.

"I've lost track of her." I hung my head. "Sorry."

"Sorry is not going to find her."

Please don't cross your arms and tap your foot at me. Please!

A shuffling sound caught our attention as a young lad around nineteen or twenty staggered up to us holding his ribs and upper abdomen with both arms as best he could. A nest of french fries was visible through the hole in his stomach.

"Are you virgins?" he asked.

The old lady snapped, "Who the Sam Hill are you and where is your Guide?"

"Come on!" he snapped back at her. "Where are they?" Speaking loudly like that must have hurt because he backed off a little. "Do you guys have any Pepto Bismol or anything? My stomach hurts."

He moaned as he massaged his stomach area with his right hand. His left arm was still pressed against the ribs on that side, that hand flattened against the area below his collarbones. A fry fell out of his stomach and landed at his feet.

"Come on. I blew up that building for the cause and I'm not even a *mahz limb*. I'm not even religious. I'm just looking for the virgins. You promised."

The old lady looked at me from under her eyebrows while she asked him without looking at him, "I'm guessing this was online you read this? And where you signed up?"

"Yeah. So?" He winced. "Ow."

The old lady and I turned to face him and together we said:

"You can't believe everything you read on the Internet."

"Yeah? Well yooze guys can go to hell. Ow."

The old lady and I looked at each other, looked at him, looked at each other again, nodded. "You got that one wrong, too." The old lady giggled when she said it. I didn't think it was particularly funny because that's exactly where we now were. The suburbs of it at least.

The old lady told the lad to "skedaddle" then turned to me with her hands on her hips, a frustrated sigh coming from way down deep inside her.

"You seem to know me," I said. "Who are you?"

"You can call me Muriel. Trevor sent me. Apparently, you're having trouble with your Charge." She shook her head. "I can't believe this. Who trained you anyway?"

She knew as well as I who had trained me and that I'd lost track of Vivie. I tried to change the subject. "Muriel, eh? Is that your real name?"

"Close enough. So, where is she?" This was a demand, not a question. "At first, I thought Trevor was full of it, as usual, but I think he was right about you. You're a handful. Let's get going before she gets in any deeper, shall we?"

She reached out to grasp my upper arm and I felt a gentle snap of power go through me and the most beautiful odor of cloves and cinnamon filled my nostrils.

"You said your name's Muriel?"

"Would I lie to you?"

Eleven

<u>Section Four</u>

I HAD NOTHING TO LOSE so I decided that Muriel probably knew best about this section and I followed her into the huge empty space that surrounded us. Behind me, I sensed the close presence of the young man with the damaged stomach and sore ribs. He was nothing if not determined.

Then *BANG.* "Ow."

I twirled around to see his face flattened against an invisible barrier.

Before I could step back to see if I could be of assistance, Muriel stopped me. "Don't worry about that. Happens all the time here."

"What happens all the time here? There's a barrier there. Why didn't we run into it?"

"It's not there for us."

"I think you'd better explain."

Muriel moved her head close to mine as she stretched her arm out to point into the distance. "See 'way down there? At the far end?"

"I see vast areas of nothing. And no, I don't see an end."

"Exactly."

I had never thought of myself as being particularly slow at

catching onto things, but I was lost. I had no clue what she was talking about.

"You seem at a loss," she said almost kindly.

"That's because I am."

"Close your eyes."

I closed them.

"Now imagine thousands of cages without bars but with only… Let's call it a force field."

I grunted.

"Remember those early *Star Trek* episodes?"

"After my time, I'm afraid."

"Ah. Right. You did miss a lot, didn't you?"

"Don't remind me."

"Open your eyes.

I did and saw what could only be called row upon row and level upon level of boxes upon boxes each with a single individual in it.

I even spotted Weird Hair and pointed at him. "Didn't take long for you guys to get him into a space."

Muriel shook her head. "Wasn't us."

"Then wh—? Ah. They do it to themselves? Isolate themselves from every single thing imaginable? Wow. That must be…"

"Absolute hell?"

I nodded.

"I'm assuming your next question would be, why doesn't it affect us?"

I nodded.

"Have you ever painted yourself into a corner?"

Muriel was such a sweet old lady. "Not until just now. Losing my Charge."

She wrapped an arm across my shoulders and led me toward the back of Section Four.

Twelve

<u>Section Four</u>

As we trekked across a morphing floor—floor?—that I couldn't even begin to understand the workings of or what it was made of, we passed enclosures of many sizes and scenarios. Most of the enclosures had only one individual in them and nothing but that one individual. No furniture, no windows, no doors, no apparent source of food or water or music or communication. And the worst of it was that they didn't seem able to see each other.

I was so busy gawking at all of this, I didn't see Linda running toward us until she was almost on top of me. She had obviously escaped from George's goons.

"Linda! What's going on? Are you OK? Where are your cheerleaders? They have Vivie."

Linda threw her arms around me and hugged me really tightly then stepped back quickly with a silly grin on her face and a shrug of her shoulders. "Sorry."

"It's OK," I reassured her while pushing her away. "I'm a hugger." I brushed myself off.

Muriel stepped in to loosely embrace Linda, but I think it was more of an excuse to prevent her from running away while being admonished. Muriel's comments were almost growled.

"It's been forever, young lady. Where have you been? No, wait. I withdraw the question."

Linda wrested herself from Muriel's long arms to respond to my questions. "I swear those girls have never, ever had an original thought in their heads. Soon as I got away from Joey and his boys and found them, and told them what I wanted them to do, they tossed away everything George had told them, and like the silly little sheep they are, they—"

"And? And?"

"And I made them take Vivie to The Mazes. It's better than here for her. Right now, at least."

"Anything's better than here." In an attempt to appear like I understood even a tenth of what was going on, I smiled over at Muriel. "Right, Muriel?"

"With a few exceptions." Muriel grabbed my arm again. "We'd best be off. The Mazes sap energy like nobody's business."

"Wow, Linda. You're actually not so bad. I always thought you were kind of a… You know, a…"

"A rat rear?" suggested Muriel as she and I stepped away from Linda.

I wouldn't have put it quite like that, but yeah, a rat rear.

"I'm not a bad person," Linda said. "Not really. I got distracted by what I thought was love. That makes it almost forgivable. Wouldn't you agree?"

"Happens to the best of us, I suppose," said Muriel. "You coming?"

"I'm certainly not going back to him, that's for certain."

Muriel caressed Linda's back as she encouraged her to step forward in the direction we were heading. "And you don't have to, dear girl. He has tossed you aside, so this means you're free. You are officially on vacation. Or retired. Whichever way you want to look at it."

"You mean…" I looked back and forth from Muriel to Linda. "You were George's Guide?"

"It was just one of those things, like the old song says."

"Well, now that you've had your trip to the moon on gossamer wings," said Muriel with more than impatience, "I hope you've learned your lesson?"

Head down with embarrassment, Linda nodded.

"And lucky you," continued Muriel, prompting Linda to raise her eyebrows at her. "We don't have time for me to give you a lecture."

Linda threw me a relieved grin that was short-lived as Muriel hadn't quite finished yet.

"That'll have to wait."

Then, as though we were a pair of grandchildren, Muriel snagged each of us by a hand and off we went. To where, I had no idea. I'd never heard of The Mazes before and told her so.

"That's my girl. Always complaining about something even when you don't know what you're complaining about. No wonder Trevor finds you difficult. Personally, between you and me," and turning to Linda, "this includes you, too, I think Trevor is nothing more than a good talker. Lazy as a frog on a lily pad waiting for a bug to fly into his mouth." Then to me again, "I like that you're your own person, not like these ones coming up." She let go of our hands to smooth her dress and fluff her hair. "Take note for future reference, ladies. Don't ever let one of your Charges get to this state."

"What state is that?" asked Linda, appearing somewhat scared. She latched onto me.

We all hurried past what appeared to be a waiting room where dozens of elderly people sat silently, no one speaking, no one moving. One of five young women would call out a name and one of the elderly folks would get to his or her feet and shuffle into one of five rooms with the young woman, to emerge a few moments later to sit among the others again.

"They just keep doing that over and over?" I asked. "Blind obedience?"

"Like my girls," put in Linda. "Mindless adherence to what the community demands. No questions. Just follow the leader. Do what you're told. Do what's expected of you. If you have a differing opinion, don't dare keep it inside your head to mull over just in case you accidentally let it come out of your mouth and change something for yourself or others. That's why some folks call this whole area Choiceville. Because nobody ever makes another one once they're here."

"It's the way folks were raised to be in small communities back in the day." Muriel ushered us forward. "It was a survival method. Hey, Linda. You used the term *mindless*. What do you think of this group?" She pointed to a gaping cave entrance in the side of a mountain that hadn't been there two seconds ago. "Think anyone in there will ever choose to plain old turn around to save themselves?"

As Linda and I peered into the cave, our shoulders touching, a bright light behind us threw our shadows onto the far wall along with the shadows of hundreds of people of different sizes —adults and children—all staring at the wall before them like it was a huge movie screen but showing only their silhouettes.

Everyone oohed and awed and pointed at our silhouettes, but no one turned around to see what was creating them.

"These people were taught this is reality," offered Muriel. "Those silhouettes are their reality."

Linda cried out loudly enough to make me cringe. "Look," she said. "Isn't that the kid George had?"

"Yeah. So where's her Guide, Dougie, then? Do you see him?"

"No."

Linda's aura flickered pink for a fraction of a second. *Really,*

I thought. *She's not telling the truth about something.*

"Ladies," interrupted Muriel. "We can't go saving everybody. We're on a mission, remember? We must find Vivie? Before she gets too disoriented? Too fatigued to care anymore?"

Ignoring her, Linda rushed into the cave dragging me along with her.

After the initial shock of being in a totally unexpected area of Section Four, I felt something comforting and warm about being in there. I could get to like it real quick. I watched the silhouettes of myself and Linda bending over Little Bald Girl.

It wasn't easy, but I was able to tear my eyes away from the silhouettes on the back wall to speak to the little girl. "Hey, kid," I said. "How'd you get here?"

"This pretty lady." She hugged Linda. "She told me to go in here. It's nice in here, isn't it?"

"When?" I asked Linda. "When did you get time?" My suspicions about Linda rose even further.

Although Muriel was still outside, she wasn't about to be left out of the interrogation. "Why here?" she yelled in.

"What better place?" Linda was now facing the wall, too, to watch the silhouette people. "Nobody has a clue what's going on out there behind us." She leaned toward me and whispered, but loudly enough for Muriel to hear, too. "For example, our little friend here has forgotten about Mommy Dearest and has detached herself from that dangerous anchor."

"*Mommy Dearest*? How do you know about that movie? It was after my time so certainly after yours."

"Come on. I'm not THAT old."

"Yes you are 'Joan.'"

"That's not funny."

"Yes it is."

"Ladies. Are we going to get about the business at hand or wait around until everybody in Section Four dissipates? Huh?

Turn around and look behind you, little girl."

"Oh heavens, no. I'm not allowed. I know what will happen to me if I do. I'll get a hole in my head like that boy has."

"Which boy?" I asked.

"The man showed him to me."

I glanced around at the crowd, but I didn't see Weird Hair anywhere in here.

"When? Where?"

Linda, ashamed: "George brought her to Section Three when all that mess was going on."

"Seriously?"

Little Bald Girl said, "The boy with the funny hair has his own room here. We saw him. Can't they give him anything? He said his head hurts. When I was hurting a lot, they gave me something to make it go away. Why can't they give him something?"

"That's how I was able to get her away. During all that chaos, Georgie Porgie didn't notice we were gone until it was too late."

"Why can't they give him something?"

"Listen, sweetheart." Linda leaned down, hands on knees, in front of the girl. "When he did what he did to get here, he made a decision to be all by himself. He put himself here. Nobody else did. When you're all by yourself, nobody is there to help you. In any way."

"I don't believe you. I'm scared. I have to stay here. They said."

"You're allowed to leave, honey," said Linda. "Because I put you here. Not you. But you'd better be quick about it. We all had better be quick to leave. You with us, Susan?"

I nodded with reluctance. Like I said, I could have gotten used to the place very easily.

"Why do we have to leave?" asked the girl.

"Don't argue, sweetheart. And where is your Guide?"

"My what?"

I tried a tactic that usually worked on most Charges: "We need your help. Please."

We hustled the girl to the entrance where she was somewhat surprised at seeing Muriel.

"Who are you?"

"I'm Muriel and we don't have much time."

"We don't," I said. "I have to find Vivie and get her to safety."

"Vivie?" The little girl turned to Linda. "That's that nice girl I saw before?"

"One and the same."

"She's lost?"

Muriel, Linda and I nodded.

"OK. I'll help."

"But where's Dougie?" I demanded of Linda. "*He* should be looking after her. Not us." I spotted Muriel's raised eyebrows. "I mean I don't mind and all. It's our responsibility to help others when we can…"

Muriel's eyebrows were still waiting.

"My first responsibility is to my own Charge. My only concern with helping others is the possibility of being distracted for too long a time which might jeopardize the well-being of my Charge." Yes, I had pretty much memorized the pamphlet Trevor a.k.a. Pete had given me during training.

The eyebrows waited.

"What?"

The eyes moved quickly to the little girl who stared open mouthed up at Linda.

"Oh."

I took the little girl's hand and placed it in Linda's. "You guys are now a team." I looked at Muriel again then took the little girl's other hand in mine. "We are ALL a team off to help someone in distress." With my free hand I reached for Muriel.

Muriel's eyebrows returned to where they should be and she managed a slight smile.

"OK, everyone," I said. "Off we go."

The little girl skipped along between Linda and me as though she were off on an exciting—safe—adventure down a yellow brick road, or at least the equivalent of one.

"So, Linda," I asked. "Are you going to answer my question?"

"Which one?"

"Where's Dougie?"

"Do I have to?"

"Yes."

"Held captive."

"Seriously? Captive? A Guide? By whom?"

"Who else?"

"Seriously?"

"Stop saying that but yes, seriously. George managed to incapacitate him back in Section Two."

The girl tugged at my arm. "My special friend needs help, too? He's called Dougie? He never told me what his name is. He's nice."

"He's a good guy," I said.

"Oh, wait." The little girl stopped walking. "Dougie didn't decide to be alone, did he?"

"No, honey," said Linda. "He didn't. He must be missing you terribly."

"I'm starting to miss him. I can feel him worrying."

"Have you ever been in a maze?" I asked her.

She shook her head.

"They can be fun," I told her. "But it takes a lot of figuring out to get through one."

"I can do it," she tossed back at me. "My name is Sophia. It means wise."

A silly grin lit Muriel's face. "I couldn't have set this up better myself."

Thirteen

MURIEL KNEW EXACTLY HOW TO get to The Mazes so we were there in no time.

But getting there and knowing what to do when we got there were two different things and I think all four of us, not just me, soon realized this. I had told Sophia that mazes were fun. I didn't know this from personal experience, only from hearsay. Not exactly a fib, I know, but not exactly the truth, either. Stretching for what seemed to be miles in both directions, a perfectly pruned and impossibly thick hedge rose above us.

"Beautiful, isn't it?" said Muriel, letting her eyes caress the hedge. "It's made of yew."

Linda said, "Aw, thank you" at the same time I said, "That's very sweet of you, Muriel."

I continued. "But how can that be? Is that yet another weird thing about this place nobody informed me of?"

Sophia giggled.

"What's so funny?" I asked her. "Linda's really pretty." I fluffed my hair and grinned at her. "And I'm not that bad either really. In a dim light."

Still giggling, Sophia said, "Not you, yew."

"What?"

"Not y-o-u. It's y-e-w."

"Oh," I said. "I've heard of that tree."

"Did you know," continued Sophia, "that every part of the tree is poisonous except for the berries. But even the pits inside of the berries are poison."

Who was this kid, anyway? "How do you know all that? You're just a kid."

"Well," she said with a sad face, "when you're stuck in a hospital bed with tubes coming out of you and going into you, it's not like you can go outside and play or anything. You have a lot of time to read."

Ah.

"Help me get this out of my arm." She tugged at her IV apparatus.

"Wait, wait," said Linda, stepping in. "I know how to do that."

Linda leaned over Sophia's arm and plucked out the IV. "Hey. Where did your teddy go?"

"I left Doctor Ted back in the cave with the shadows. I don't need him anymore. I have real friends now."

All three of us said "Aw."

"Maybe some little girl or boy will find him comforting."

As Linda and I exchanged glances, Linda's knuckle dabbed at the corner of her eye and she said, "This kid is gonna kill me."

"Trevor's gonna kill *me* if I don't get Vivie out of here." I put my hands on my hips and spread my feet wide as I looked up along the top of the hedge then along its length. "Any ideas how to get in there, Muriel?"

"I think I hear people talking," said Sophia. "Lift me up."

"Up where?"

"Linda's the tallest one so you guys help get me up on her shoulders."

For being a scrawny, sickly young girl, Sophia was surprisingly agile and we had her standing on Linda's shoulders in no time. From the front, Muriel held her ankles and from the back, I held her calves.

"You all right up there?"

"Hey. I see her. *Hey! Vivie! Vivie!*" Sophia began waving with wide swoops which nearly made her lose her footing and my tenuous grip on her calves.

"Whoa, whoa. Easy, easy," I told her.

"Yeah, but it's her. *Vivie!*"

When I heard Vivie's voice, an involuntary gasp issued from my chest. *Oh. Thank you, thank you.* "Ask her where she got in."

"*Where'd ya get in?*"

Silence. I assumed Vivie was pointing because Sophia's head turned to the right and she rose slightly up on her feet.

"Easy, easy," I cautioned again.

"*How'd you get where you are now?*"

I could hear Vivie's voice but her words were somewhat muffled for me through the hedge, but it was clear that Sophia could hear her just fine. "*Great. Thanks. Stay there. We'll come and get ya.*"

Loud protests from Vivie. The word "No" was easy to hear through the hedge.

"*It's all right. It's all right,*" yelled Sophia back to her. "*These ones are friends. These ones are good people.*"

I lost my grip on Sophia when she bent down to wrap her arms around Linda's neck and throw her legs out. "Let me down, let me down. We gotta go. She's running away."

"Is she alone?"

"She has those three girls with her. She called them her sore-a-day or something like that?"

"Sorority." The corners of Linda's mouth turned down.

"Yeah. That's it," said Sophie who was already about fifteen feet down the hedge to the right. "She said the entrance is here."

We followed Sophia to an opening that was arms akimbo wide and which faced another hedge. Corridors went both ways.

"Which way?" I asked, trying not to let my worry about Vivie show.

"Left," said Sophia immediately, and she stuck her left hand out to touch the hedge on that side. "No matter what, no matter how long it takes, and no matter how silly it might sound, we have to keep our left hands on the hedge at all times as we go. It's the only way to get through a maze."

"Seriously?" I asked. But Sophia was already turning a corner.

"Hurry," she called back. "You can run faster when you're scared, and she's scared."

Trust me, I was probably more scared than all of us put together. I hurried.

Fourteen

The Mazes

Sophia was right. It didn't take us long to get through The Maze. For me it was an eternity, of course, but I think it took perhaps fifteen minutes at most. Like I said, we don't have any need for timepieces on this side of The Veil, so that was more of a guess than anything.

When we exited the end of The Maze, my fears were not lessened. Quite the opposite. There stood the three cheerleaders beside George and Joey and the other goons. Vivie was nowhere.

"Where is she?" I demanded. "What did you do with her?"

With his thumb, George, grinning like a Cheshire cat with rabies, pointed behind himself to a narrow thicket of scraggly bushes, so untidy and uncared for, they looked almost hairy, almost animal-like. I think it was another maze, but this one went straight back as a single corridor then took a sharp turn. From what I could remember of my high-school geometry, the turn was called a right-angle. I think I gulped.

Because she was closest to me, I grabbed onto Muriel's upper arm and yelled to the others, "Let's go, team!" I pulled Muriel along with me, but George and Joey stepped in front of us to block our way.

"Not so fast, ladies. You'll upset the balance."

"BALANCE?" I yelled at him, and I think some spit flew out of my mouth when I said it, but I didn't care if George got any of it on him. "Balance, schmalance. What stupid balance are you talking about?"

"Hope you're up on your physics, Sandra."

"Susan. Her name's Susan," Sophia informed him with her eyes in slits. "You're being very rude to her. Stop it." She moved in close to me on the other side from Muriel.

"Thanks, kid," I said. "I can handle the likes of him."

"Maybe so," George said. "But I'm willing to bet you won't be able to get your gal through *this* one."

"If I do? What are you betting?"

"What am I betting? I'm betting you won't."

"Let's go, team." And I snagged Sophia's hand with mine. Her grip was firm. She was as determined as I was to save Vivie.

Muriel leaned in to whisper to me. "He's right, you know. We can't go with you. I remember now. There are only two allowed in this one at a time."

I didn't bother to whisper back. "And why is that?"

To Muriel, George said, "You wanna tell her, or shall I?"

Muriel shrugged. "I just managed to get her to be civil to me, so I'll let you do it. Georgie Porgie."

"Two. One Charge. One Guide. It's all to do with balance. And brains. Brains, as well. Maybe some arithmetic. Lots of physics. There are tricky spots in there. Dangerous spots. Spots that might pop either of you into your own world like you saw back there in those boxes—or, I guess, they're more like non-boxes. Right?"

What could I say in response to that? I had no clue what he was talking about.

"Even fiery places where you—or your Charge—will burn to a crisp and blow away with the slightest draft."

I still couldn't think of anything to say. My mind was

reeling. Was Vivie in there? How far in was she? Was she in any kind of trouble yet? Or was I already too late?

"And she doesn't trust you, remember? She's running away from you, remember?"

I remembered.

Muriel pushed my hand from her arm and rubbed my shoulder. Sophia let go of my other hand and moved around in front of me to give me a hug that was a lot stronger than I could have imagined coming from such a skinny wee thing. Looking down I noticed, too, that her hair had started to regrow from its shiny round skull. Even Linda came up and brushed her cheek against mine.

"We'll find a way to help you," whispered Linda. "I promise."

I whispered back from the corner of my mouth. "I've got a feeling I'm going to need all the help you guys can give me. And then some."

My team stepped away from me, and through the entrance that led into the hairy corridor I went.

From behind me, Sophia called out. *"Susan! Whatever you do, don't touch the sides in that one though."*

I stuck my head back out of the entrance. "What am I in for?"

"I know what they are now. They're mesquite bushes," Sophia said. "I didn't like reading about them because they're kind of scary. They have big long stabby thorns. You can see the thorns better up at the top there." She pointed. "Where the bush thins out like skeleton fingers. See?"

She waited for a nod from me.

"These guys use up all the water in the ground and that makes other trees die and that's why some people call them devil trees."

Oh, great.

Fifteen

The Mesquite Maze

WITH AS MUCH COURAGE AS I could muster, I stepped onto the mossy pathway centered between those tall, vicious bushes. I was no sooner past the first turn to the right inside those scraggly walls of thorns than I found out what George meant by arithmetic and physics. Here, I'd say maybe three steps in, the pathway changed from moss-covered earth to metal tiles. These tiles were not quite three of my feet square, and on the Earth Plane I wore size 8 shoes. There were narrow spaces between these tiles. Half an inch maybe? And space on their sides, too.

From the moss-covered ground I stepped onto the first metal tile. It rattled, and it swayed a little bit like a weight scale does, but so far so good. The next tile was a corner tile that would be my turning point into the corridor there. I couldn't see beyond it. When I stepped on this corner one, a great *BANG-BANG* made me cover my ears and squeeze my eyes tight.

When I opened my eyes, the tile that I would have been stepping on next was gone as was the one I had just stepped off from. As I leaned over to look into the emptiness, a bead of perspiration dropped from my forehead to disappear into the darkness. I wasn't sure if it was my imagination or not, but I could have sworn I saw a tiny orange glow way down below.

Enough of that! Let's get to the business at immediate hand. I could see that the tile on the other side of the open space was held by hinges of a sort. The hinges looked strong, so I knew they were the same as the ones holding up the tile I was on. I'd be safe for now. I hoped so, at least. Looking back to where I had stepped from, I gauged that I would have been able to jump back and onto the mossy pathway and escape this dangerous place. I would have if I hadn't heard a desperate whimper. I raised my eyes to the far end of this new corridor.

There she was! It was Vivie!

"Vivie! Vivie!" I called out. "I'm here. I'm here. Don't move. Stay where you are. I'll…" Um. I would what, exactly? Jump over this gaping hole and maybe trigger that next tile to plunge me into the abyss below? Perhaps trigger Vivie's tile to snap down, too? I could now see that she was probably in the same predicament I was in because the tile on this side of her was missing and I could only surmise that she was staring down into emptiness at the corridor's turn there, too. I could tell she was as terrified as I was.

"Stay there, Vivie. Don't move. I'll… Well. I'll figure something out."

Great. Just peachy keen great. She wasn't listening to me.

Then a familiar voice from the other side of the mesquite bushes to my left. It was Muriel. "Hold on, Sandra."

Another familiar and welcomed voice came through the mesquite bushes. "Her name is Susan. Why is everybody so mean to her?"

Then Linda's voice: "Can you hear us, darling?"

I replied in the affirmative all the while hoping I hadn't gone insane under the stress of the situation and was merely imagining rescue.

A moment later, from farther along the outside of the hedge: "Hang on." Linda's voice again. "Oops. There you go, sweetheart. Y'OK?"

A Sophia-giggle turned my face up toward the skeleton-like branches of the upper bushes about four tiles farther down the corridor. The top half of Sophia teetered there.

"Whatever you do, don't fall forward, kid."

Sophia laughed and spread her arms outward like airplane wings. She burst into song: "Near, far, wherever you are…" The theme song from the movie *Titanic* was well after my time, but that didn't mean I hadn't heard it here. It was a beautiful song and well-executed, both by the original songstress, and now, by Sophia.

"Don't mess around, Sophia."

She grinned down at me, then her face went all serious when she looked over at Vivie.

Muriel's voice asked a question and Sophie replied with: "Yes, I can see them both. But I can see Vivie better."

An excited muttering from Muriel brought forth another response from Sophia.

"But there are empty spots in front of her and beside her. She can't go anywhere."

This I heard clearly from Muriel: "Dirty old bean bags and rat rears." And I saw a bright flash of angry orange through the hedge. "I know what this is about. Stay where you are, the both of you." A pause, a flash of deep green, the color of teaching and learning, a combination of intellect-yellow and love-blue. "Can you both hear me? Can you hear me, Vivie?"

Blessed be all the powers of the Universe but Vivie turned to the sound of Muriel's voice and said, "Who's that?"

I wasn't sure if a breeze blew through the hedge to make that shushing sound or if Linda had done it, but the next thing I heard was Linda's voice, full of relief. "Hi there. It's Linda here. Remember me? I think you probably will remember the little girl you tried to save? That's her. Up there. Is she looking up at you yet, Sophia?"

"Yeah. She is. Hi Vivie. Whoops." Sophia's enthusiastic wave nearly toppled her into the thorns at the top of the mesquite bush.

Vivie frowned. "She looks different."

"I'm still me," Sophia laughed, pointing at her arm where the IV tubing had been. "There's still a little hole in my arm. See? But the bruise is gone."

Linda's voice came through the hedge. "You can either trust us or stay there forever. Your choice, Vivie."

"I don't know. I'm scared. This place is weird. Beyond weird. And there's somebody at the far end staring at me."

Muriel's voice. "Excellent! She can see Sandra."

Sophia, Linda and I laughed together as we shouted, "SUSAN."

Vivie didn't laugh. But although we were over fifteen feet away from each other, Vivie made eye contact with me. "But she looks familiar. Sort of. Maybe." She glanced up at Sophia then back over at me. "You remind me of somebody I used to know. Sort of. I thought she said her name was Petunia but that was my rabbit's name. When Petunia died, it was my first experience of that kind of thing, so I must have gotten mixed up."

"My name is Susan. I'm going to do my best, with the help of my friends, to get you out of here."

I wasn't certain, at that distance, if a corner of her mouth turned up in a semi-smile or not, but when Sophia whooped a YIPPEE, I was reassured that it hadn't been my imagination.

Sixteen

The Mesquite Maze

SOPHIA DISAPPEARED FROM THE TOP of the hedge so quickly, I thought she had fallen off Linda's shoulders. Then I both heard and sensed movement on the other side of the hedge, to my right now, and was nearly slapped on the face with the end of a huge piece of white cloth.

I heard Linda laughing so hard she could barely speak. "A corset? You… ha ha… You wear a corset, Muriel? That's hysterical!"

I knew the ensuing grumble had to be from Muriel.

On closer examination, the huge piece of white cloth was Muriel's flowing gown and it now lay across the top of the hedge and on top of it, appeared Sophia.

"I'm going to jump down," she told me. "You have to catch me."

Before I could respond, or even wonder how to prepare for this feat, she was in my arms then at my side tugging the thick white cloth down off the top of the hedge. She plucked a few thorns out of it and flicked them into the abyss.

"Now tie this around your waist and then around mine."

She glanced up at me with such a worried face, I realized that my mouth was wide open and my eyes were probably bulging. I relaxed.

"You don't have to look so scared. I don't weigh much."

I still couldn't say anything.

She adjusted my knots then hers. "It's in case I fall? I won't go all the way down?"

"Uh. You mean… You mean you are actually planning to do what I'm afraid to think you're planning to do?"

Through the hedge came Muriel's voice: "Just do what she tells you. We're calculating jumps over here."

"*WHAT?*"

"Susan. You have to trust her and trust me, too."

Had Muriel just used my real name? Yup. Sophia was planning to do what I was afraid she was planning to do.

Linda's voice: "It's going to be OK, Susan. Really it is. We have it figured out. Pretty much."

"Pretty much? That's reassuring."

"Yeah, yeah. Try not to worry."

Muriel interrupted with, "Don't say things like that. You'll only make Vivie worry more and… Well, whatever."

Great.

I looked down at Sophia when I felt her easing me to the outer edge of the tile we were on. Like an Olympic sprinter, she crouched, swaying forward and backward before making the leap across the gap to the tile beyond it where she scooched over to one side to make herself small.

Her grin took up half her face. "Your turn."

I knew if I thought about it, I would mess up, so I just did it. I leaped, landed and felt the tile wobble for a second or two under us before a tremendous *BANG-BANG* announced the return of the tile behind us and the disappearance of the tile in front of us.

"See? It's easy, isn't it?" Sophia smiled up at me, all innocent-like. "Now. Don't do anything. It's Vivie's turn."

I called out to Vivie. "You know what to do now?"

"Yes." And she leaped out of my field of vision.

BANG-BANG!

A tile on this side of where Vivie had been, appeared, and the one she had been on became blackness.

"Well?" I listened but heard nothing. "Vivie? Don't do this to me."

"I did it. I'm safe. I did it!"

I don't think I was supposed to hear what Linda said next because she more or less whispered it: "See? I told you it would work."

"Shh. She'll hear you." Then Muriel's next comment made a shiver run up my back. "Sorry I doubted you, Linda. I'll get you that banana split when we get back."

I think I heard a high-five slap but didn't want to believe that's what it was.

"Excuse me?" I said through the hedge. "You made a *BET* whether this was going to work or not?"

"Don't worry your pretty little head about it, Sandra. It worked, didn't it?"

"If I get out of this alive I am going to kill both of you. Painfully."

All smiles, Sophia took her Olympic sprinter pose again. "This is fun, isn't it?"

"Sure, kid, sure. Oodles of fun."

Sophia made the leap and once she had made room for me, I followed.

BANG-BANG!

The tile we had been on disappeared as did the one ahead of us.

"Your turn, Vivie," I called out.

"*NO! WAIT, WAIT!*" came the voices of Muriel and Linda.

Then Muriel's voice: "Vivie has to jump back one, I think."

"You THINK?"

Sophia spoke up. "Yes, she does, Muriel. We have two empty spots in front of us. The second one is right at the turn so there's no way we can move forward."

I called out to Vivie. "Are you getting all this?"

BANG-BANG!

Then Vivie's excited cry as a tile came up in the corner. "It worked!"

"All right, Vivie," said Muriel. "Take another turn."

"You two are just guessing out there, aren't you?" I was getting annoyed. My flight or fight instincts were battling each other, and I didn't like it. Not one little bit because I couldn't do either one. If I didn't end up with PTSD after this, I was immune to it.

"Linda has made a delightful little drawing. We're going by that."

I didn't reply.

"It's working, isn't it?" That was Linda.

I didn't want to admit they were right, so I didn't. Instead, I took a deep breath. "Give it a shot, Vivie. What have we got to lose?"

I heard her laugh. I heard the *BANG-BANG.* Then her whoop of victory.

We jumped to the corner tile.

BANG-BANG!

"Your turn, Vivie."

BANG-BANG!

We jumped.

BANG-BANG!

Vivie was now three tiles away from us, with one empty space and one tile between. She was facing a corner empty space.

"Wait a minute. Wait a minute," I said. "I think you're going to have to step back one again, Vivie."

She turned to face us.

"One wrong move and we'll be setting off tiles the wrong way."

Vivie called out to Muriel and Linda. "Now what?"

"Don't make a move until we figure this out," Linda said.

I slipped my arm across Sophia's shoulders more for my own reassurance than hers, I think. "I guess we wait, huh? By the way, Vivie, how did you get to that second corner in the first place? Didn't you have to jump over empty spots?"

She smiled at me. "Ever watch that Ninja show on TV?"

Sophia brightened. "Yeah, it's cool what those guys can do, eh?"

I drew a blank on that one. "Oh, please. Do fill me in."

"It's a reality show with really difficult obstacles to go through."

"A reality show."

"Not like a soap opera or anything like that. It's with real people doing real things."

"OK."

"Well, on the Ninja show there's always one obstacle that has these wobbly platforms of all sizes and shapes and you have to run across them without falling off into the water. It looks really hard. All of it does. But those guys have inspired me to look ahead at the future, to be brave in the face of danger, never to accept my own limitations but to boldly go where no one has gone before."

Yep. This girl was a writer, all right. "So…?"

"So I held my breath and ran."

From outside the hedge: "OK. We have it figured out now."

"What's next? Vivie's turn, I think, eh?" suggested Sophia.

"You are right, sweetheart." Linda continued: "Vivie steps back to bring her corner tile up. Then she needs to jump to that one right away. Let's see how that works."

Let's see how that works?

Sophia giggled up at me. "When you roll your eyes they almost disappear inside your head, you know."

"Thanks."

"It wasn't a compliment. It's creepy."

"Thanks."

BANG-BANG!

BANG-BANG!

"Woohoo. I made it!"

Beside me, Sophia did a fist-pump and held her palm out to me. My responding high-five was not all that enthusiastic.

"Look," I said.

Three spots lay between us and Vivie on the corner tile: one tile, one space, one tile, then Vivie's tile.

"Hey ladies," I called out to our engineers on the far side of the hedge. "Should we move one tile? Um. *See how that works?*" I didn't bother to even attempt to keep the sarcasm out of my voice.

Muriel replied with, "That should work but make absolute certain you both step on that tile at exactly the same time. I think that's what George was talking about when he said only two at a time. You and Sophia now count as one."

Sophia and I snuggled together with our arms around each other. I took a deep breath. She said "One, two, three. Go." And over we stepped.

BANG-BANG!

"You made it?"

"We did."

"I think we need to do that once more," I suggested.

No one objected, so Sophia and I repeated our combined step to the next tile.

BANG-BANG!

Sophia and I received a thumb's up from Vivie and an are-you-guys-all-right from the other side of the hedge.

"We made it," I assured them.

Vivie turned away from us then, and as she looked down the next corridor, she let out the loudest blood-curdling scream I'd ever heard in my life.

"What is it? What's wrong?"

"There's a… There's a… I think it's a… I think it's a… a yeti?"

"A what?"

Sophia, once again—the little bookworm!—helped me out. "It's also called an abdominal snowman. Um, I mean an *abominable* snowman."

A laugh escaped me. I couldn't help it. "Describe it. Please."

"It's really tall and it's hairy and it's white and… Wait a minute."

"What?"

"It could be a…Yes, it's a polar bear. But…"

"But what, but what?

"It's changing again."

"To what?"

Vivie's laugh elicited one from me and from Sophia as well. "It's a giant teddy bear right now."

Good grief. "Dougie! Knock it off."

Dougie's laughter boomed along the corridors all the way to Sophia and me. "You're almost there. But don't make any sudden moves. Listen to me."

"I'm listening."

"What we need is for this young lady in the corner to jump into my arms."

Vivie's head snapped over to look at me. She didn't say anything, but I knew she had too many questions to start asking them right now.

"Go ahead," I assured her. "You can trust him." Then in a louder voice I asked Dougie, "Why, though? What's your reasoning?"

"She's got an empty spot to jump over. If she lands on me instead of the tile that's under me, she won't trigger any reactions from the tiles."

"Sounds good to me. So far. Then what?"

"Then she'll be safe, and I'll see what I can do about you and my Charge. Hey, Sophia! It's me. How ya doin'?"

Sophia's eyes were soft, innocent, smiling when she looked up at me. "Is that my friend I was telling you about? He got away from the bad man? He's all right?"

"He is indeed."

Sophia clapped quietly and didn't quite jump up and down with joy but bounced ever so slightly beside me.

"You ready?" I heard Dougie say.

"I am," answered Vivie and she leaped out of sight from me.

"Gotcha," I heard Dougie say. "Now what you need to do is go over there and hope we can get your Guide and my Charge out safely, too. OK?"

"You mean that girl named Sandra is my—"

"Susan," called out Sophia and I heard two voices from the other side of the hedge say it, too.

Was I finally getting some respect?

Sophia did her Olympic sprinter thing and I followed her onto the corner tile. When she saw Dougie, she beamed with the sweet innocence that only a child can. He reached out his arm from across one tile and she grasped his hand. He lifted her over the tile easily onto his tile where he undid her end of Muriel's big white dress. There he turned and eased her away to the side. I imagined it was onto *terra firma*.

I slung the rest of Muriel's dress over my shoulder and took the Olympic sprinter crouch.

"Here goes nothin'," I said as I closed my eyes and leaped toward Dougie.

I felt strong arms enfold me and lift me away to settle my feet on solid ground. I heard Vivie and Sophia laughing and when I opened my eyes, Dougie had morphed into a yeti again.

"Oh, stop showing off," I said, laughing, relieved beyond belief.

He placed a long, hairy arm around Sophia and said, "Hey, if you've got it, flaunt it. Right?"

She giggled.

Then Dougie became Dougie again and turned to me. "I've got a feeling all this business isn't over yet. Am I right?"

Behind me, Muriel appeared. "You are right about that, my boy. Unfortunately. Here, gimme that." Roughly, she untied her dress from around my waist and wriggled into it.

"A corset though?" I teased.

Muriel pointed her index finger at me with her thumb up like it was a pistol, and looking all the way down its imaginary barrel, she whispered. "What happens when you judge somebody? Sandra?"

"I guess it depends if they deserve the judgment or not," I shot back.

She fluttered both hands in the air. "I'm gonna kill him. I'm gonna kill him. He always hands off the difficult ones. And I've been stuck with more than one of his castoffs."

Dougie cleared his throat. "I think we'd best be moving on?"

"Any idea what's ahead of us?" I asked.

"I would suggest you withdraw that question," Muriel offered. "Susan."

Great.

So I withdrew the question about what was coming up next and I'm glad I did. If I'd known, I probably would have run away screaming.

Nah. Who was I trying to kid? Er, make that *whom* was I trying to kid? There goes my internal editor, the harbinger of reasons to be afraid of what was coming up next. We'd somehow gotten ourselves into Section Five. Toad poop and toad pee, too.

Seventeen

<u>Section Five</u>

HOW APPROPRIATE. A TEAM OF five to deal with Section Five. I always thought coincidences like that were especially creepy. "Does anybody know how to get out of here?"

"How about a beam-me-up-Scottie?" snapped Muriel.

"A what?"

"Never mind. It was after your time."

"Well, if it was after mine, it was most *certainly* after yours."

"Ladies? Ladies?" Dougie put in his two cents' worth, too. "I believe you are supposed to be planning some sort of escape and not bickering among yourselves?"

"*Between* yourselves. There are two of us. So it's *between*. Among is for more than two." I caught Linda's eye roll even though her lids were closed. "Sorry. When I get nervous, I—"

"Yeah, yeah. We know *aaaall* about it, Sandra. Shall we get down to business? Linda? Take notes."

From the folds of her Joan Crawford dress, Linda pulled out a notepad and pencil. As she flipped to a new page, I spotted crude diagrams of the tile maze Vivie, Sophia and I had just navigated from. "Shoot."

All business once again, Muriel waved us forward up a rocky hill.

I knew before we got to the top of that hill and saw the smoke and fire in the caldera below that we were in trouble. I knew by the smell that we were about to face a volcano. A collapsed one with all its workings bubbling below.

"P.U. What stinks?" asked Sophia, flapping her hand in front of her nose.

"I would hazard a guess that it's sulfur," I informed her. "And that means there's a volcano around somewhere. Probably up ahead." Then I added, "Where Muriel is leading us. No doubt to our certain deaths." This last comment elicited no comment from Muriel. At least not one that I was able to hear.

"Well, actually," put in Vivie. "Sulfur itself has very little odor. It smells awful when it combines with other elements, particularly hydrogen to produce hydrogen sulfide. It… What?"

We had all stopped walking and were staring gobsmacked at Vivie.

"How do *you* know all this stuff?" Linda asked her. "The kid here reads a lot, but you too?"

Vivie shrugged. "I dunno. I guess."

Sophia beamed up at her. Birds of a feather.

"Wow," was all Linda could come up with.

"You didn't have any friends to play with either?" Sophia asked Vivie.

"No lollygagging, now. Let's keep moving. We want to get past this mess before dark."

"I'll be your friend," Sophia informed Vivie as she grasped her hand.

"Ditto."

"What's ditto mean?"

"The same. It comes from the Latin through Italian, Tuscan dialect to be exact…"

As the bookworms bonded, my mind drifted away from their conversation to what might lay before us. And like newly hatched ducklings, we followed Muriel to the top of the hill where we once again stood gobsmacked.

What lay below us could only be described as a mixing bowl made of mountains with a well at the bottom burping up a stench so fierce it made my eyes water.

"Dante did a good job describing this," said Vivie to no one in particular. She coughed.

"Dante? Who's Dante?" asked Sophia.

"He wrote a great big long poem about the nine circles of Hell."

"He got the count wrong," said Muriel. "There are only seven. But his description was correct. Who has scissors?"

"Scissors? Seriously? You expect one of us to be carrying scis—?"

Smiling, Linda waved a pair in front of me.

"Start cutting." Muriel spread open the skirt of her dress as though she intended to curtsy to royalty.

No one moved.

"We need to make something to cover our mouths. I think this reeking horror is toxic, is it not, Vivie?"

A nod from Vivie as she bent to help Linda snip strips of cloth from the bottom of Muriel's dress, removing enough to almost show her corset. Dougie and I helped wrap the home-made scarves around each of our faces.

"Can't we go back?" I asked. "Maybe go around?"

Tugging down the remains of her robe to cover the tops of her thighs, Muriel pointed up and behind us where the floor of what looked from here like a building jutted out from one of the mountains. From where we were standing, I could see the sky through a familiar set of right-angled rows of square holes.

"The corridor of tiles? How did it get up there?"

Muriel's glare told me don't ask. I guess she didn't know. "That's where you came from and it's the only way back. As you can see, trying to go through there will get you down here again. And a lot faster."

"Just thought I'd ask. Onward we go then?" I adjusted my face scarf. "What are you doing?" Linda was drawing in her notebook.

"Up here we can see the best way to get around the worst of it. I'm drawing a map. Down there, we won't be able to see the path."

"Path?"

"Over to the right there? Alongside that second mountain?"

"That narrow little ribbon?"

"It won't look so bad once we're there."

"It's called perspective," added Vivie, no doubt thinking she was being helpful. She wasn't.

Eighteen

I DON'T KNOW HOW WE did it, but we all managed to work our way through the smoke and stench to the far side of the bowl of mountains. "I will be eternally grateful that the most horrible experience of my life, both here and before here, is over with."

"Me, too," said Sophia, shaking out the strip of cloth we had wound around her mouth and nose. "You guys are all dusty." She began brushing off Vivie's shoulders with the strip of cloth. "Turn around."

Vivie turned to let Sophia brush the dust from her back. I stepped in to brush off Sophia's back and Linda brushed off mine.

Without being asked, Linda produced needle and thread from yet another of her mysterious pockets and quickly basted the strips of cloth together to repair Muriel's robe. "When we get back, I can do a better job of this." Linda adjusted a fold.

"Is it just me or did it suddenly get cold?" I shivered. "Or maybe it's 'perspective' from nearly being cooked to death getting past that cauldron then suddenly back to normal?"

Vivie returned my grin.

I know I was reluctant to climb the last little bit to the top of the final mountain, being afraid of what may lay on the other side of it, but seeing the others fall in behind me without any enthusiasm whatsoever, I knew I wasn't the only one.

"Move it along, people. Move it along." Was Muriel getting more and more bossy? Or was it nerves?

At the top of the hill, we paused to take in the scene. On the right was a forest with a path leading into it. This forest was nothing like the bush of mesquite thorns we'd had to maneuver, it looked like a real forest. A normal one. And a testament to my opinion on that was a huge blinking neon sign. Yes, a blinking neon sign that flashed

THIS WAY TO BLISSLAND

"Looks like this is where we part company with the team," Dougie told Sophia. "Blissland is where we're going."

Sophia tossed the rest of us a sad smile. Then Linda, Vivie, Muriel and I hugged her.

"You're the best friends I ever had," she told us. "I am going to miss you. Especially Vivie. But especially you, too, Linda. You were really good to me. You saved me from the bad man."

"Oh, but Linda's going, too," Muriel informed us. "She has graduated."

"Yay!" Sophia jumped up and down, turning in circles, arms high before she slapped a high-five with Linda, then with Muriel.

Vivie and I stepped forward and after my "Come on," she high-fived with us, too.

"And as for you two…"

I felt my shoulders tighten.

Vivie sidled over to grab onto my arm. "Look at that. Is that where we're going next?" She pointed to the left now. "It's beautiful but we aren't exactly dressed for it, are we?"

I took in the scene where acres of land as white as the fleece of Mary's little lamb stretched toward the horizon. Waiting down below us, like lambs in wolves' clothing, were seven Huskies harnessed to a large sled piled high with blankets and supplies.

"Seriously?"

"Welcome to Snowland," Muriel informed us.

"Snowland. No doubt another one of Trevor's original naming ideas?"

"Mine, actually."

"Sorry."

"Don't be. It's lame."

"Apt though."

"It is. Let's go. Goodbye Dougie. Goodbye Sophia. We'll all probably run into each other again. And I know you and I will for absolute certain, Linda."

"Do you really think so?" asked Sophia, her face brightening.

I responded this time: "Happens just as often here as it does on the Earth Plane. Maybe more so. You can pretty much bet it's gonna happen eventually."

"Awesome!"

"It *is* awesome, isn't it? Safe journey, you guys."

Beside me, Vivie imitated my wave. "Yeah. Safe journey, you guys."

"Don't forget about that banana split you owe me, Muriel."

"I won't." Muriel turned to us now. "Let's get this over with. Brrr. I hate the cold."

When we got to where the dogs were, they all stood up and practically wagged their butts off with what was either the excitement of seeing us, or the excitement of knowing they were about to start a run. Maybe a combination? Sure, why not? I always like to look on the bright side.

I had no idea how to operate a dogsled and told Muriel so.

"You don't know how to *do* very much at all, do you, Sandra? Happens when you spend all your time reading instead of the actual doing of things."

I don't know whose grin was more sheepish, mine or Vivie's, but we shrugged at each other, then simultaneously asked Muriel what she needed us to do.

Her instructions were explicit: "Get into those sweaters, hats and jackets and get onto the sled and under those blankets. You will need sunglasses, too."

We had no sooner gotten settled in under the blankets and slipped on our very dark sunglasses, when a loud scream from Muriel, "*MUSH!*" made both Vivie and me cover our ears. The dogs took off at full gallop.

What can I tell you about our trip back to the Section One intake area? I saw nothing but snow upon snow upon snow and the curled-up tails of our furry taxi drivers working like windshield wipers. I soon fell asleep with the smooth rhythm of sled on snow and stayed that way until the jar of the stop and the excited barks of our canine engine announced our arrival.

Yes. Section One. That's where we were heading. Since Vivie's introduction to this part of our world had been interrupted there, we had to start over at that point. I had no problem with that even though a few thoughts about Hiram passed through my mind. Was he still believing he had seen a vision of the devil with purple hair wearing a tank top with Grumpy Cat on it? Or had he accepted that life goes on here, too, and that surprises were always the norm when different cultures, eras and ages were tossed together in the same bag? It wouldn't be long before we found out.

Nineteen

Entrance Tunnel

I WAS HOPING, FOR VIVIE'S sake, that we might run into Eduardo and Maria when we got to the Community Center again. It always makes it easier when Charges' challenges are shared with other Charges. Makes it easier on us Guides, too. But first, Vivie and I had to wend our way through the entrance tunnel.

"Are you feeling up to doing this?" I asked. "Not that you have a choice, but…" I paused for a reaction, got none, so continued. "It will be interesting to find out what you, uh, 'envision' this time around on the way through the tunnel. Last time, if you recall, it was a high school corridor."

"Yeah. With some creepy-looking kids in it." She patted her hair and straightened her tank top. Grumpy Cat glared out at me. "And then George and everybody got us totally off track."

"It shouldn't take too long to get through this time. George and his gang are probably looking for us back at the cal—"

"Don't say 'probably.' Use the word hope. Probably is wishful thinking. Hope springs eternal and it's a necessary element for maintaining sanity."

This kid was getting good. "Um. Sure. Uh, yes, let's *hope* he's still looking for us back at the caldera. Where did you get all *this* positive psychological information from, anyway?"

"From Sophia. What comes after the tunnel?"

"Section One. And I would recommend you not conjure up a lynch mob when we get there this time."

Her laugh was full on, right from her stomach. Another good sign.

"Were those guys in the lynch mob real?"

"Hiram's real. He's the one you scared. Not sure about the other guys. Anyway. Here we are. Deep breath."

She took one.

"Ready?"

She nodded.

We stepped into the entrance tunnel and that's all it was. A tunnel.

We joined hands and as we ran, we passed several sad individuals in worn-out clothing sitting there either on rocks or directly on the tunnel floor; some were standing but not many. I could tell we barely registered on their conscious minds as we went by.

"Who are all those people? They look so sad. So lonely."

"I suppose they were expecting something other than what's here so they're waiting for things to change to their expectations."

"I was never good at riddles," said Vivie. "Can you explain?"

"Maybe later. We're here."

From the tunnel's end, we burst into a world of sunshine and fluffy white clouds and fields of grain and hedgerows of trees separating them. In the distance sat the Community Center. I pointed at it.

"Yes, I remember." Vivie stopped running and so did I. "Everything is so beautiful here. So bright."

"Did you ever hear that old Christian hymn, 'All Things Bright and Beautiful'?"

She shook her head.

"Even if you had, so therefore think you're imagining all this, you're not. It really is like this. Hey. Look!" I pointed at the Center again, specifically the front door. "Recognize anybody?"

"Hey. It's that guy who tried to help me when those men were trying to kidnap me to lynch me. What's his name again?"

"Eduardo."

"Yeah," she smiled. "Eduardo. He's really cute."

"You like him."

"Yeah. And isn't that your friend with him? That lady there?"

"You can see Maria?"

Vivie looked up at me. "Why not?"

Ah. Things were looking up in a most fantastic way if she could see another Charge's Guide at this level. Now if I could keep things status quo, my task would—

From behind us came a shuffle of clothing and a gasping of winded woman as Muriel practically plowed into us. "I can't believe how rat-rear rude you two are. You left me behind in that horrid tunnel with those… those… unbelievably stubborn people with their endless questioning."

"Those dudes talk?" Vivie threw a wondering shrug in my direction.

Muriel grabbed my forearm to balance herself as she bent over trying to catch her breath. "You never think of anybody but yourself, do you?"

I pointed at Vivie with my free arm. "I'll have you know—"

"And I will have you know that I will not allow you to say such cruel things to my dear companion, Susan. She cares deeply about me."

Still bent over but turning her head, Muriel sputtered, "Oh, you writers. Always so dramatic with your words." Then she plastered a wide smile on her face and rose to full height, suddenly—and may I add mysteriously—recovered from her breathing issues. "Well, now. Who do we have here?"

Maria nearly knocked me over when she ran up to throw her arms around me. "Welcome *back*, Petunia. Welcome back. You guys made it *through*. Hoorah."

Who says hoorah anymore?

Over Maria's shoulder I could see Eduardo grinning at Vivie and getting a shy, sweet-girl smile back.

Excellent!

"C'mon, let's get to the Community Center. I simply *must* hear absolutely *everything* about your *fabulously* exciting journey." Maria hadn't gotten any less dramatic—or controlling—in my short absence. And she hadn't gotten any weaker either. She practically dislocated my shoulder when she jerked my arm pulling me along behind her at top speed.

I laughed to imagine the look on Muriel's face when Maria yelled out, "I can't wait to hear how you met the old lady in the corset."

"You can see it?" I asked.

I knew Vivie and Eduardo were close on Maria's and my heels and Muriel was trailing behind them so could hear every word.

"Thought I caught a glimpse of it through that patched up mess of a robe she's wearing," returned Maria. "And she got so out of breath earlier? What else would it be?" She winked at me.

I wasn't wearing a corset and *I* was getting severely out of breath being dragged along with Maria. I think Maria knew Muriel much better than she was letting on.

"So what *happened*? Did George hunt you down like he said he was going to? The big meanie."

"He did."

"Did he do anything… Anything bad?"

"He did."

"Ooh. What?"

"D'you mind? I can't talk and run. Not all of us… were athletes… on the Earth Plane… y'know."

"Ah. You're just excited to be back on track. That's all. Here we are."

And so we were. And who was blocking the steps to the porch? You guessed it. George and his goons and Linda's three backup cheerleaders.

Toad poop.

Twenty

"WHAT DID YOU DO WITH Linda and my little bundle of fresh energy? How dare you take them away from me. Believe me, you are going to pay for what you did, and pay dearly. I am not going to forget this."

"Ooh, I'm scared."

"Don't antagonize him," Muriel whispered into my ear between out-of-breath gasps. "It will make him even more annoying. If that's possible." Then to Vivie and me, "Come along now. We can't afford to linger."

"I'm so happy to be back here starting over," Vivie announced to Muriel and me. "It'll be so much easier here."

Maria and I exchanged glances.

"Um. Well. Not so much," I informed Vivie. "This is where things can get both tricky and sticky. What's going to happen is—"

"Whoa, Nelly." Muriel actually covered my mouth with her hand. "She has to figure it out by herself. That's in the very first chapter of the manual."

I grabbed Muriel's wrist and pulled her hand away. "I know. Near the bottom of page 2."

"Ah. So Sandra has actually read some of the manual. Good

girl." No smile accompanied this snarky comment. She pushed a cheerleader aside and ascended the steps of the porch to the entrance door of the Community Center. She swung the big door open and propped it with a straight arm against it.

"What are you guys talking about? Figure out what myself?"

I glanced up at Muriel and got a nod of approval to continue. "That, too," I said.

"Well, how am I supposed to figure out what I'm supposed to figure out without—?"

George stepped forward now, puffing his chest out. "These dudes are constantly doing this kind of thing to you new folks." He shuffled closer to Vivie now, thus making Eduardo slip his arm around her waist to pull her back a step. "They like to thwart thtuff, stuff."

Behind George, one of the cheerleaders giggled. His glare did nothing to stop her, instead, it made the other two join in behind their pom-poms. Were Georgie Porgie's fans losing respect for him? Interesting.

Muriel's fingers drummed against the entrance door. "Sandra?"

"Oop, yeah. OK. All right. Hey, uh, Vivie? Break the spell and let's get moving." I took her by the arm opposite from Eduardo.

"But what's he talking about? I want to know. It concerns *me*, doesn't it?"

"It does, but let it go."

Maria joined Muriel on the porch to help hold the big door open for us. I noticed that they didn't bother to introduce themselves to each other. Curiouser and curiouser.

"That means you, too, Eduardo," Maria urged. "Hustle."

If I had disliked George's grin before, I disliked it a lot more now as he semi-whispered to Vivie. (Creepy doesn't anywhere near cover it.) "You can always meet me later to find out."

I shivered. "Vivie. Snap out of it."

"Eduardo. Come on! Now!"

Between Eduardo and me with urgings from both Maria and Muriel, we got Vivie up onto the porch and through the entrance into the main hall.

Whew.

Twenty-one

<u>Community Center</u>

As we stepped into the Center's large foyer, a round of applause erupted from the dozen or so smiling people standing there. From among them, and the only one not smiling, Trevor stepped forward.

"Well done, Sandra. Thank you, uh, Muriel. Your job is done. I'll take over again from here."

Muriel crossed her arms. "If it's all the same to you, 'Pete,' I'm going to stick around. I'm quite enjoying myself with these two. You were right. Never a dull moment." She actually smiled.

Trevor opened his mouth but just as quickly closed it. He turned away toward the back of the huge open building whose columns at the far side led into the mixture of gardens, grocery stores, convenience stores, houses, restaurants and other buildings with dark alleys between most of them.

"Up to you," he tossed back at Muriel. "Up to you. But she's a handful."

"Well, how about that?" I grinned. "La di dah. I feel like a rock star with people vying for my company like this. And I'm a handful. Ooh. Maybe I'll make it into the next issue of *'Teen Magazine*.*"

Maria hugged me. "Sorry. Ain't gonna happen. Long defunct

mag, my dear." She waved Eduardo away from Vivie's side. "Unfortunately, we'll have to see you guys later. Meanwhile, break a wing, huh?" Off she went, with Eduardo nearly tripping over his own feet as he walked along beside her but without tearing his eyes from Vivie.

"We need to get going, too," I told Vivie. "The sooner the better."

"Where to?"

"This is where it gets tricky. Because the choice is absolutely one hundred percent up to you."

Twenty-two

We hit Patates restaurant where all three of us, Vivie, Muriel and I soon demolished a dish of poutine each. It was Vivie's idea, I'd never had poutine before, but I'd heard of it: fries and cheese curds with gravy. In my day—listen to me with "in my day" like I was thirty or forty years old or something. Anyway, in my day, our mothers did the cooking, and nobody much ordered in or went to restaurants except for special occasions. Besides, poutine was still pretty much restricted to the Province of Quebec in Canada and only making inroads to the rest of North America by the mid-1960s, which was when I left the Earth Plane.

As Vivie and Muriel finished up the last of their poutine, I found myself drifting. Fries, cheese curds and gravy had triggered a memory. A sad one. Where had I last seen poutine? Ah. Trevor a.k.a. Pete. Yes. I had seen him here in Patates just before everything fell apart and here he was again, but now alone and smiling at a half-full dish of poutine at the empty chair on the other side of the table.

I leaned toward Muriel. "What's he doing?"

She smiled at me. "Lizzie finally clued in to what Trevor was really telling her when he would say: 'Whatever you do, don't try to find out what food is a substitute for.' You were here. You heard him."

"How do you know what I heard or didn't he—? Hey. Wait a minute. What name did you guys cook up for this section, anyway, huh?" I held the palm of my hand up toward her. "Wait. Do I want to know?"

"Comfort-Land."

I felt a blush creep up my neck and spread to my cheeks. I hoped it wasn't showing but when Vivie, a worried look on her face, asked if I were all right, had I eaten something hot, I knew the whole world could see it. Then my mother's voice chipped in: *Stop exaggerating, Susan.* OK, so not the whole world, just maybe everyone in Patates? All right, all right, Vivie and Muriel were the only ones who could see it. Probably the only ones who cared.

"Let me guess," I said to Muriel. "Like us, Trevor isn't allowed to actually *tell* anybody—even us, for example—what exactly to do, so he must resort to tricks to get us thinking along certain lines?"

Can a smile be sarcastic? "And she read not only the first, but also the *final* chapter of the manual, I see."

"I used the expression myself: 'tricky and sticky.'" My blush faded. "He's not so bad after all, is he? He wasn't being mean to poor Lizzie. He wasn't forcing her to eat. He was doing his best to make her realize why she wanted food so much." I glanced over his way as my mind flew through what I always referred to as its files, trying to conjure every single annoying thing he had ever said to me. There were too many to count.

I felt Muriel's comforting there-there pat on my shoulder.

"Thanks," I said. I suppose there's no worse moment than the one in which you discover that the very person you thought was being as mean as possible to you, was doing the exact opposite. They were doing it—dare I use the term *for your own good*?

"Oh! How could I have been so wrong about Saint Pete? How can I make it up to him? I'll never forgive myself!"

"Whoa, whoa, whoa, whoa! Don't do that. Don't do that. You'll pop yourself back over to the caldera if you go all guilt trip on yourself."

"What are you guys talking about?" Vivie pushed her dish away, dabbed at her mouth then plopped the napkin on top of her empty dish. "You're kinda scaring me." She glanced around. "Where's that Maria lady?"

I managed to snap out of my funk to suggest, "You sure it's Maria you're looking for?" My laugh was, yes, as mean as Trevor a.k.a. Pete's had ever been at me for being less than honest. Vivie was going to dislike me as much if not more than I had ever disliked Trevor before we got out of here. And my position required that I not let that bother me. That was going to take some work.

"Hey, Pete," I called over at him.

His satisfied smile—I would have normally called it a smug smile—did not change or diminish when he turned toward my voice.

"Thanks, huh?"

I got a thumb's up before he rose from his chair, snatched up the partially eaten dish of poutine, and headed toward the re-cycle bins. As he walked away, I saw a brief flash of halo over his head. Brief, but there.

I couldn't resist. I hollered out, "Seriously, Pete? A halo? Seriously?"

Beside me, Muriel laughed. "Don't get him going."

"Does this mean…?"

"It does. Trevor has finally managed to get rid of you." Muriel's giggle was not in the least comforting. "This is wonderful, isn't it?"

From the corner of my eye, I could see Vivie's open-mouthed stare, but I ignored it.

"Wonderful for who? Whom. Me or him?"

Muriel rose from her chair, patted her hair and brushed off the front of her gown which was now miraculously untattered again. "Why, for both of you, of course."

I rose from my chair, too then, patted my hair and brushed off the front of my tie-dyed T-shirt. "Of course." I hauled out my love beads from under my shirt.

"What are you guys talking about?"

Amused eyes boring into mine, Muriel bobbed the top of her head toward Vivie. "Well? Are you going to answer the girl?"

Lucky for me, my dear friend Maria chose that very moment to show up with Eduardo. I was the one who embraced her in a bear hug this time. "Vivie was just asking about Eduardo."

"No I wasn't," Vivie grunted as she was hugged by Maria. "Oof, you're strong."

Both Muriel and I simultaneously placed our hands on our hips and turned to face Vivie as Maria stepped away to whisper something to Eduardo.

"Yes I was."

Eduardo beamed.

From behind him, Maria, frown creasing her brow, mouthed at me, "What's going on?"

I pulled Maria aside. "Poutine is way, way too tasty."

"Yeah. So?"

"So… how's your Charge coming along? Think he's strong enough to unstick the stickiness of Comfort-Land?"

"I think so now. I'm pretty sure. With your help. And Vivie's help."

"That will go both ways."

"I know. You owe me big time, remember?" Maria turned away from me. "While you deal with tidying up after your meal, I'll go catch Trevor and bring him back."

"No need."

"What do you mean there's no nee—?" I swear her happy gasp drew in half the oxygen in the restaurant. "Oooh. REALLY? You graduated to a new *Guide*? You really *did*?"

Once again, I was subjected to a bone-crushing hug.

Twenty-three

Comfort-Land is the most difficult area to escape from and I don't think I need to explain why, but I will anyway. Comfort-Land is what many of us, while on the Earth Plane, were taught was Heaven. Here, everything you ever liked and loved was available usually by merely thinking of it, except for wishing for actual people and pets, of course, because these had control over their own selves, not us over theirs. Of those we loved who were still on the Earth Plane by the time we arrived here, their draw on us was like that of the Moon on the tides; you might call their love and grief and missing us "anchors," great big, huge, heavy anchors. Those who had passed on before us had either already skedaddled by the time we got here, or were in an entirely different "Comfort-Land." Comfort-Land was pretty much one's own making. Please note that I said "pretty much." I didn't say entirely. There were forces at work in every single section on this side of The Veil, and scary to say, most of them were of our own making but we weren't aware of this.

I knew that Vivie's favorite things, her tablet, her cell phone and of course poutine and rocky road ice cream (who couldn't love rocky road ice cream; even if you had allergies, it was almost worth death for) and those cute little kitten earrings that her grandmother had given her when she turned thirteen, were not currently on her mind because she was still taking in this new world, but it wouldn't take long before she began to reach for them only to find them missing from her life.

Next thing I knew, Vivie was digging around in a huge purse.

"Where did you get that?"

"It's my purse."

Maria and I exchanged glances. Muriel wasn't anywhere near involved in the current situation to help me out because she was concentrating on a young couple in a heated dispute at a table at the far end of Patates. My quick take was that Husband/Boyfriend wanted desperately to put ketchup on his fancy *cuisine-français* beef tenderloin, and Wife/Girlfriend thought this more horrifying than setting fire to a newborn puppy. Welcome to Comfort-Land! It appeared Muriel found this to be immensely amusing as she was wearing a Trevor smirk. I turned back to the issue at hand.

Eduardo was watching Vivie. Were males subconsciously attracted to females with large purses? Perhaps only to what might be IN those large purses out of pure curiosity and wonderment, with maybe a little self-preservation thrown in there?

OK, Susan. Stop doing writing research and get to work here. "I realize that but where did you get *your purse*?"

"It was on the chair. There. Where I left it."

I turned toward the table we had recently vacated after our delicious meal of poutine to see one of the cheerleaders in a Patates hat and apron wiping up after us. That meant George had to be close by.

"George is here," I whispered to Muriel.

Muriel pulled herself away from the drama at the far end of the room, shrugged and plucked a bit of nonexistent lint off her robe. "You know what that means."

Indeed, I did. "Vivie? Drop the purse and come with me."

"What? No way." She cuddled the purse to her chest.

Eduardo moved to her side and placed a firm hand on the shoulder farther away from him, to hold her in a semi-hug across her shoulders. "She doesn't have to."

He could see me. This was good and not so good at the same time. Back-up is always nice when we're going through difficult times—like being ordered to hand over our purse—but when back-up turns into *folie à deux*, shared madness, it's not so peachy keen anymore.

"Eduardo," I said. "She has to leave her purse behind."

Vivie hugged it closer. "No way. Everything I need is in it."

"Then list the contents," I demanded.

Eduardo released his grip on Vivie's shoulder to step toward me. Oh, he was such a darling, so handsome, so elegant. So gallant. How I had dreamed to have a boy like this when I was on the Earth Plane. I envied Vivie, but not all that much right at the moment. Right at the moment, I had to convince her to dump the purse and get moving out of this neighborhood, out of this section, out of Comfort-Land and into the next level. Sure, yes, there was nothing physically dangerous here. No fiery calderas, no thorny mesquite, no lynch mobs—well, that remained to be seen, but you know what I mean, right?

I calmed down and so did Eduardo.

"My cell phone. Charger. Money." With her right arm up to the elbow inside that monstrous bag, she resumed rummaging. "Let me see. Lipstick. Bunch of pens." She held up three in her fist to show me. "Every writer needs pens." She put them back inside the purse. "Breath mints. Um, tissues, tampons." At this last mention, she blushed. "A bottle of liquid bandage, safety pins. Looks like two. One's a spare, I guess." She smiled over at me. "Comb, toothbrush and paste. I forgot about most of this stuff. Shall I continue?"

I shook my head. I well knew what women carried in their purses.

"Moisturizer…"

I had been guilty as well. Ask Trevor a.k.a. Pete how long it took to get me to realize this was the last place anybody needed to carry anything around with them.

"Well hello, people."

… except for maybe a sledge hammer. "What now, George?"

"Vivie's purse is divine, isn't it?"

"It's a knock-off."

"Actually, it's not." Like a kid imitating a magician in a grade school skit, George fluttered his fingers at Vivie's purse.

"Toad poop."

"Rat rears," added Muriel, now with her full attention on my problem with Vivie.

Vivie's purse sparkled even in the low lighting of Patates.

"There we are," George said proudly. "Instant Louis Vuitton. Wanna try for a Chanel?"

"Stop it right now! And Vivie, OK, I concede. Sling that monster of a purse over your shoulder and follow me. Eduardo? Maria? Muriel? Shall we?"

As one, we marched out of Patates into the evening darkness of Comfort-Land's endless avenues and alleys.

Behind us, George called out: "You are no fun at all, Susan. No fun at all."

Watch me, I muttered to myself. *Just watch me.*

"Hey, what was that?" Vivie asked. The hand not struggling to keep her purse on her shoulder shot up to cover her eyes. "I just saw a big flash of red. Am I OK? Did something happen? Am I seeing spots or something?"

From my right-hand side: "See what you started?"

Maria, on my left, appeared to be more understanding, but

with her, I could never tell for a hundred percent certain if she was being sarcastic or kind. "Wow. Your aura's energy levels certainly didn't diminish during all that kerfuffle you went through in the numbered sections." Her trademark guffaw didn't make me feel any cheerier. "That was quite the blast of righteous rage." She poked me with her elbow, giggled, then hugged me.

"What's with the hugging all the time now?"

"I missed ya. I was worried about ya."

"Well… If it's all the same to you…" I brushed off my tie-dyed T-shirt and straightened my love beads.

"It isn't. But I'll try to control myself." Another guffaw.

We followed Vivie and Eduardo, who were holding hands, along a wide sidewalk. It hadn't really dawned on me before, but there was no actual roadway. No vehicles of any kind moved along in the dark shadows beside the walkway. I guess Ferrari-Land was in another area. I didn't want to wonder what was within those shadows, though, so I refused to let myself think about it.

It wasn't much brighter ahead of us because the streetlights here didn't give off much light. I suppose everything and every-body in this section tried to conserve energy, or were running out of energy. I didn't notice him until Vivie stopped in her tracks with a startled little gasp.

Sitting on the sidewalk with his back to *Cose*, the local Italian-run dollar store, was Joey. And Joey was in trouble. There was no empty soup can or open pouch sitting on the sidewalk in front of him, but I knew he was desperate for something. I could tell by the fear and sadness in his eyes.

"Just a little bit, please. I've never felt so weak. So very tired."

As we caught up to Vivie and Eduardo and semi-circled around Joey, too, I knew he recognized us. There was a brief flash of something in his eyes, but immediately he tried to hide it from us, and I must say he did a decent job of it. But still, I knew. I knew he was on his last legs and would soon dissipate and the strangest thing was, I didn't know if that would make me sad or not. I mean, I knew the guy. Well, I'd met him. Did that make him a friend? Someone I should care about? I still don't know the answer to those questions.

"I know you from somewhere," said Vivie. "Don't I?"

Joey's smile was sad as he looked up at her. "I'm sorry, young lady, I don't think so."

"Yes, yes. I remember now. You and Linda and those other guys and those girls were all friends. I remember. Why can't you remember? Are you sick? Is there something we can do to help you?"

Vivie squatted down in front of Joey letting her purse swing around in front of her onto the sidewalk. She opened it and began to dig through it.

"I'm sure I have a twenty in here."

"It's not money I'm needing." Ever so slowly, Joey stretched out shaking fingers on the end of a skinny forearm.

"Don't touch her," I said. "Don't be like him."

As though his hand weighed a hundred pounds, Joey let his arm go and his hand landed on the sidewalk beside his thigh. "He didn't say a word. He just walked away from me, and when I tried to follow him, he pushed me hard. Right here." With great effort, Joey raised his hand once more to touch his chest. "Right here. Where my heart is. He pushed me. I think he broke it. My heart, I mean."

Muriel stepped in closer and even though she whispered it, I could still hear her, and I think the others did too. "You know what you have to do, Joey. Don't you?"

"But what if he needs me again? I can't go. Not without George."

"But look at you," I said. "You're almost out of energy. Have any of the people passing by helped you? Doesn't look like it. And we can't help you either."

Vivie was still elbow deep in her purse, but she took the time to glance up at Eduardo. "What are they talking about? Why won't they do anything to help him?"

"I am as astonished as you are, not only from seeing Joey here in such poor condition, but that no one is willing to help him." Eduardo turned to Maria. "Please inform me as to what is going on here."

A rarely seen sadness washed over Maria's face. "There's nothing we can do. Really. There isn't. It's Joey's own making."

Vivie pulled a crumpled twenty from her purse and set it on the ground in front of Joey. "I hope this helps a bit."

Before any of us could react, Joey's hand reached for the twenty, but diverted to grab Vivie by the wrist.

She screamed.

Eduardo whirled around to rip Joey's hand from Vivie's wrist. "*AIEEE!*" Eduardo cried out. He released his grip on Joey's hand then leaped back, rubbing his own hand. I could see the mark on his palm. Not from heat, from cold.

I leaped in to free Vivie's wrist then wrapped both my hands around it in an effort both to soothe her injury and to restore the energy Joey had sucked from her body.

Tears formed in Vivie's eyes and her lower lip began to quiver with the realization that she had been duped by someone she was trying to help.

"He was trying to…"

"Yes," I said. "He was trying to kill you."

"… kill me."

"It's called the second death," Maria threw at her as if the concept meant no more than having a second helping of mashed potatoes with cheese at a Thanksgiving dinner with family. "Are you OK?" She leaned in to pick up Vivie's purse for her. "Oof.

What'cha got *in* here? Rocks? Oh wait." That hearty guffaw again. "You do, actually." With her index finger, Maria tapped at several of the diamonds that encrusted Vivie's exquisite purse. She laughed again. "I had a friend," she winked at me, "who used to say 'my purse is worth more than what's in it.'"

"Ha ha," I said.

"But it's still a knock-off. It's a George, not a Louis."

Vivie rose to her feet and dusted herself off. "I can't believe it. I tried to help him and…"

"It's his own doing but he won't accept that. Here."

When Maria handed Vivie's purse out to her, Vivie took three steps back, flailing her hands at the purse. "I don't want it. I don't want it. I never want to see that thing again. Give it to him." She pointed to Joey who seemed to be almost fusing into the bricks of the *Cose* dollar store. "He can have it and everything in it." I'd never seen her eyes so wide.

I pointed at Vivie's purse. "That's coming with us."

"NO WAY!"

"Yes way. As you said, there are many items in there that might prove to be of value to us in future."

"Like WHAT? I know it's bad. I don't know how I know, I just know."

"Nevertheless, it's coming with us. And you're going to be doing the lugging."

"Atta girl, Sandra. You tell her." As usual, no smile accompanied Muriel's comment. "And since you appear to have gained such great insight into our current dilemma, how about you tell us where we are going next."

"No problem. I know exactly what we're going to be doing and where we're going."

"As if." Maria laughed as she slipped her arm around Eduardo's elbow. "How about carrying the young lady's purse for her for a while, my gallant young Charge?" She turned back to me, "I can at least get us to the town limits. Follow me."

So once again, we were a group of five skipping along yet another brick road to who knew where.

Twenty-four

Outskirts of Comfort-Land

THE TREELESS OUTSKIRTS OF COMFORT-LAND's meadows brought us to the edge of a narrow river with a few sad bushes struggling in the sand along its near shore. The far shore was solid rising forest except for a clearing behind a wooden dock of sorts that jutted into the water as though the forest was sticking its tongue out at us. The river meandered away from us on both ends so I couldn't see where it came from or where it went, especially in the dark. The good thing was it appeared to be narrow enough for even an inexperienced swimmer to get across. Depending on how deep the bottom was and how far out it went, we might be able to almost walk across. Maybe.

"So. How many of us can swim?"

"If you can, Petunia, that makes one of us," Maria said. "I can maybe float on my back and kick my way across if somebody steers me. I know *you* never learned, Eduardo."

"You never learned to swim?" Vivie's disbelief showed in her voice and most likely was what distracted her from once again noticing Maria's use of the name Petunia for me. "There's nothing like jumping into a lake from a dock anchored out in front of your grandparents' cottage. Or swimming in a river that goes through your town. I always spend half my summers…

used to spend half my summers at Grandpa and Grandma's cottage," a sad smile, "and the other half of my summers on the river with the neighborhood kids. It's awesome. Was awesome."

Eduardo's eyes were wide with fear as he stared at the river's edge. He shivered. "I cannot think of anything more frightening than going in there."

"Why?"

"When you grow up in Bolivia, the last place you want to be is around a body of water." I expected a laugh, but one was not forthcoming from Eduardo.

Maria raised her hand. "Florida here. If it's bigger than a bathtub, there's an alligator in it."

Vivie glanced at me, then at Maria then back at Eduardo who continued, "Alligators, crocodiles, anacondas, piranhas…"

"I can teach you," said Vivie, placing her hand on his shoulder and staring up into his face with so much kindness I had to turn my face away to prevent my eyes from filling with tears. "I can teach you how to swim without thinking of what might be in the water below you. We had snapping turtles. Lots of scary stories went along with those things." Vivie's smile didn't match her eyes. "Like people getting pulled down by them, never to be seen again. I used to be afraid, too, but I got over it. How about it? Do you trust me? Will you let me teach you?"

"In sixty seconds or less?" Maria put in. "Behind us."

I'm not sure they'd spotted us yet as they were far enough away. Maybe three hundred feet? And it was dark, but there jostled what I knew was Hiram's lynch mob, carrying torches instead of hoes and shovels. It looked like they were on the hunt for Frankenstein's monster this time, not Grumpy Cat on a T-shirt worn by a purple-haired girl. Under any other circumstances, it would have been exceptionally funny to see this mob in real life because of what a gal told me about the mob scenes in those old midnight horror movies I liked so much. She had studied screenwriting in college and told me that in those days, the extras were told to mutter "rhubarb rhubarb." If you listened very, very carefully when watching those old get-the-monster movies, you could actually hear the word "rhubarb" once in a while. However, since I thought I spotted the glint of moonlight, such as it was, on a shotgun barrel, there was nothing funny about *this* scene. Nothing at all. No siree, Bob.

"Can somebody please conjure up a rowboat or something like that?" I suggested, of course as a joke, but still scouring the darkness for the sign of one anyway. "A raft? An inner tube? Maybe a log?"

"Over there," Eduardo whispered. "A boat. And, *gracias a Dios*, it has a motor."

With Muriel supervising, Vivie, Maria, Eduardo and I—with Eduardo doing most of the heavy work (this guy was getting dreamier by the minute)—managed to move the old wooden motor boat into the water. It floated.

With Vivie knee deep in water and Eduardo staying one hundred percent safe on shore, they did a cursory inspection of the motor boat for leaks, or actual holes, then we all helped slide the motor boat about a quarter of the way back onto the shore.

The mob was maybe fifty feet closer.

"I think we should be all right for as long as it takes to get from here to there," said Eduardo with enough confidence to make me believe he wasn't shaking in his still-dry boots. He grinned. "We can always use Flaca's purse as an anchor." He took Vivie's purse from me and looped it over his head like an over-sized medicine bag necklace.

"Flaca?"

Maria laughed. "It's an expression of affection."

We waited.

"It's Spanish. It means skinny." Maria climbed into the motor boat. "It's nice. It's like dear, or honey, or sweetie pie."

There were three seats. Well, more like two and a half. One seat, a wide board, crossed the middle of the motor boat; a similar seat crossed near the back close to the motor. The third seat was a triangle of wood wedged into the bow. Maria lowered herself onto the middle seat and over to one side. She motioned for Eduardo to step in. He did.

"You've done *this* before, though, haven't you?" Maria asked.

"On occasion. Reluctant occasion." As Eduardo bent over, arms out, to make his way to the back seat, Vivie's purse swung back and forth from his neck, and the motor boat bobbed up and down and wobbled from side to side, making the bow dig a slight groove into the sand beneath it.

As soon as Eduardo was in his spot, Maria waved at Vivie. "You're next. And easy does it."

The motor boat made barely a bobble while Vivie took her turn and settled in beside Maria.

"Now you two have to push the boat into the water. But don't let it get all the way in. And whatever you do, don't let go of it. It's Muriel's turn next."

Maria slightly leaned back toward Eduardo and Vivie followed suit. So, because the weight was now mostly at the far end of the motor boat, the front tipped up enough out of the groove in the sand to allow Muriel and me to ease it farther into the water. When the mere tip of the bow was all that remained on shore, I said, "In you go, Muriel."

"Wait, wait." Maria fluttered one hand at Vivie. "You get back here beside Eduardo." She fluttered her hand at Eduardo now. "Scooch over."

From perhaps a hundred and fifty feet away now, a voice. Hiram's voice, "There they are." What the other men mumbled was not "rhubarb rhubarb," it was much more threatening than that. It sounded like "get the monster."

Eduardo had slid over too quickly on the rear seat so since Vivie was at that moment lifting her legs to swing them around to the far side of the seat so she could move in beside him, this made the motor boat wobble violently.

"Squat down! Squat down!" urged Maria, grabbing hold of her seat with one hand and the edge of the motor boat with the other. The motor boat settled.

"LET'S GET 'EM, BOYS!"

We managed to get Muriel onto the seat beside Maria and I pushed against the bow with all my might, trying to turn the bow around to face the other shore and climb in simultaneously. When I was knee deep in water, I slung one leg in and managed to collapse onto the bottom of the motor boat.

"THEY'RE GETTING AWAY."

As I righted myself, a loud boom and a *plink plink plink* told me I hadn't imagined a shotgun among that determined mob.

"Start the motor," Maria told Eduardo.

I could see that my push had been strong enough to make the motor boat drift, albeit slowly, toward the far bank of the river, but it was drifting sideways, parallel to the shore. I hadn't pushed it hard enough. Or maybe when I got in and fell to the bottom of the boat, I had stopped the rotation? Whatever, we were all exposed. I worked my way up onto the triangular bow seat from where I watched Eduardo lean toward the motor, raise himself from the seat slightly to look at one side then the other, then ease himself back down, a puzzled look on his face.

"Do you know how?" Maria asked him.

"Where's the button?"

Another loud boom from the shore—this one making rattling noises against the side of the motor boat. I was ready to panic. "Where are the oars? Is there a paddle?"

Vivie called out to me, "Use your hands. You and Muriel. Paddle as hard as you can."

"It's a pull-start. Get out of the way, Eduardo. I know how to do it." This from Maria.

I knew Eduardo and Maria were changing places because the motor boat wobbled like crazy.

Another boom behind us as Muriel and I leaned to opposite sides of each other and paddled with the one hand that was water-side. It didn't make a lot of difference in our speed, but it felt good to be at least trying something to save ourselves.

Behind me, Maria grunted and the slight whir accompanying it told me the motor hadn't caught.

Another boom. There had to be more than one shotgun in the mob, although intervals between the booms were long enough to indicate reload time. That guy had to be good at reloading if he was the only one with a gun. Did I care about this right about now? Not really. *Current details, Susan, current details.* And right now, one of those details was snapping turtles. I was hoping Vivie was wrong about those things. My father had taken me fishing more than once and had told me to never ever drag my fingers in the water because they might look like worms to a fish. A big enough fish to take off one of my fingers. Or all of them.

Another grunt and another whir from the end of the motor boat.

Eduardo's voice: "I think I know what you're trying to do. Let me try it. I just have to get this purse off me."

A shuffle of changing bodies, a bobble of boat, a grunt from Eduardo, a whir and a *chug chug chug whine* and the motor kicked in.

"I think I know what to do from here," said Eduardo. "I turn this thing. Right?"

He was right but I'm glad I was still holding onto the bow because he started out at full power. All five of us were nearly propelled out the back of the motor boat.

Luckily for Maria, she had managed to get herself resettled onto her wooden plank seat, but Muriel went backwards against Vivie.

Another boom from the shore was followed by what now did sound like "rhubarb rhubarb."

We no sooner had Muriel upright and comfortable than the motor coughed, hiccuped and died.

"Rat rears."

"This is what it must be like for astronauts," said Vivie. "They blast off then drift silently into orbit. This is kinda cool." She and Eduardo exchanged grins. "Just kinda. Not a lot."

Another blast from shore and the plinking of shotgun pellets landing was several feet from us now. We were still out of range. For the moment, at least.

Maria pointed to the water ahead of us. "Looks like we're moving into faster water. Where's the paddle? You said you found it, Susan?"

"No, I was asking where one was. That's all. What about under the seat?" I pointed. "See if there's anything under there, Vivie."

Maria added, "There aren't any oarlocks so it would be a paddle."

Another boom from the shore sent pellets raining down on us and bouncing around off the bottom of the motor boat. I don't think they were trying to kill us because they were close enough to do some damage by now, but weren't. We were being drawn by the fast water toward the near shore again, where the river's bend was deeper and the current stronger. The mob was keeping pace with us along a narrow pathway beside the river there. They were no farther than fifty feet from us.

"Is everybody OK?" I asked, plucking a shotgun pellet out of my hair. Nobody got hit? I tossed it to the bottom of the motor boat. Killer snapping turtles, or finger-eating fish, I still wouldn't dream of tossing lead pellets into a body of water. Speaking of which: "Hey, Maria. Is it just my imagination, or are we moving even faster?"

"I think so. Hurry up, Vivie. Is there anything under there?"

Vivie was head and shoulders under the seat when a horrific scream tore out of her and in her haste to abandon the search, she banged her head on the bottom of the seat.

Eduardo reached over for her. "Flaca, what is wrong?"

"*SPIDER!*"

Within the space of a second, and no, Mom, I'm not exaggerating, Vivie was on her feet.

Sure enough, two long hairy spider legs stirred the air before hooking onto the seat. Another leg was thrown up, another, then the inch-and-a-half-long segmented body of a dock spider, followed by its other four legs, hoisted itself onto the seat. Under any other circumstances, I would have thought this to be adorably cute. I would have imagined the spider to be saying, "Hi there. What can I do ya for?" But Vivie let out another scream and before Eduardo could stop her, she was up on the seat of the motor boat, up onto the side of the motor boat itself, and into the water, flipping the motor boat over as she went.

I could swim, and as Maria had said, she could float, and she did just that, on her back now, trying to kick to the right beat that would bring her to the now-upside-down motor boat to have something to hold on to. She was doing a right good job of it, too, so she would be OK for now.

Muriel was managing to keep herself afloat, but I knew that her heavy robe would soon become impossibly waterlogged and bring her down.

I reached for Eduardo. "Just relax. Please. You have to trust me. I'm going to turn you onto your back."

When I tried to do this, he flailed his arms.

I insisted: "No, no. Don't do that. You have to relax. You

have to trust me."

From the far shore, "I'm so sorry. I'm so sorry. You have to help him. Please."

A quick glance told me that Vivie had arrived safely to the clearing on the other side of the river where she stood dripping water.

"Let her help you, Eduardo. Let her help you."

Eduardo relaxed against my chest, so with my arms wrapped through his armpits, as calmly as possible, I swam us on our backs for the few feet between us and the upturned motor boat. He made no move to resist me. When we got to the motor boat, I got him turned around so he could hold onto the rudder. The motor had fallen into the depths of whatever lay below us. I had no wish to know what this might be.

"You guys all right?" I asked Maria and Muriel who had both managed to get themselves a sturdy handhold on the motor boat. "I have to go to my Charge." I tread water.

"We know," said Muriel. "Go."

"I'm all right," said Maria. Then nodding her head toward the spot where the river disappeared around the bend, then turning her body parallel to the motor boat with her head in that direction, she said. "Let's see if we can do this. Get a good grip and kick hard."

I heard splashing from the side of the motor boat I couldn't see. Good, Muriel was still with us.

"We'll go with the flow—" An involuntary guffaw escaped Maria's throat. "No pun intended. Don't make me laugh." More laughter. "… until we get some speed. Oh dear." A gasp, a cough. She must have swallowed water. "Then I hope we can veer off to the other side of the river." She caught her breath again. "Go, Susan, go. We'll be fine. Go."

On the far shore, I could see that Vivie had collapsed into a shivering heap. I took a good strong kick that got me about three feet from the motor boat before something bumped my head. It was Vivie's purse. Was this an omen? I no longer believed in omens, but I flipped onto my back with the purse on my chest and swam toward Vivie.

From this angle, I could see vigorous splashing, and hear Maria's breathless instructions to kick underwater. "Better propulsion that way."

The splashing stopped, and the motor boat gained speed. But with the stronger Maria on this side, the weaker Muriel on the other side, and Eduardo pushing blind from the rear of the motor boat, it suddenly veered to the shore where the mob now waited.

Twenty-five

<u>Outskirts of Comfort-Land</u>

BY THE TIME I GOT to Vivie, she was sitting cross-legged with her arms around herself and staring horrified at the receding motor boat. She was so absorbed in worry, she didn't take a second look at her purse when I set it beside her.

"Are they going to be OK? Can they get away from those awful men?"

"Maria knows what she's doing. And I think Muriel's a lot smarter than she acts sometimes."

Then Vivie jumped to her feet, pointing to the other shore. "Look! Look!"

"What?" I whirled around.

Four or five fizzling torches twirled in the river like fumbled cheerleaders' batons while Eduardo did his best to fight off the several men who were dragging him away from the overturned motor boat onto shore.

Hiram's mob had captured Eduardo. They were leading him away toward Comfort-Land. Although Muriel and Maria were tearing at the men with frantic hands, they had no effect. To the men, Muriel and Maria were nonexistent.

"No! No! We have to help him. Please. We must." With this, Vivie ran off along the dock, her dive taking her nearly halfway across the river before she surfaced with strong overhand strokes.

"Rat rears." I grabbed her purse and, at first using the dock as a handhold, I waded into the water until it was at chest level. Once again, wanting to keep the water out of Vivie's purse, with the purse on my chest, I swam on my back toward Comfort-Land, the section we had just escaped from.

By the time I got to shore, Vivie had already disappeared. I cross-body-strapped the purse onto me, then, while running into the maze of Comfort-Land's streets and alleys once more, I grabbed random corners of my tie-dyed T-shirt to squeeze as much water out of it as I could.

I was about to experience the exact same problem Maria had had with Eduardo: she had gotten him out of Comfort-Land only to have him return on a ruse of someone else's making. Maria had never explained to me what that ruse was, it wasn't any of my business; perhaps someday I would find out, but now was not the time. *Now* was his third time into Comfort-Land. Vivie's second. This did not bode well for either of them. Nor for Maria. Nor me as you can probably guess.

As I ran past the front of the *Cose* dollar store, I was saddened by the greasy stain on the brick wall and the sidewalk, all that was left of poor, sad Joey. Up ahead, by the process of sheer blind luck, I spotted Vivie paused at the entrance of Hair Today Hair Tomorrow.

"Hey," I said, as out of breath as I'd ever been. "I'll go with you." I unslung its strap from across my body and with great relief, handed the purse over to its rightful caretaker.

We entered Hair Today Hair Tomorrow.

Inside, two gum-chewing women in their sixties, one a bottle redhead, the other a bottle blonde, stopped in mid tease of their respective clients' hair to smile at us as we entered. The redhead set her comb down and stepped toward us, her impossibly high '80s' hairstyle making her close to six feet tall, and her head at least a foot and a half wide. "Five-minute wait OK with you gals?"

Without a word, Vivie took a chair and grabbed a magazine off the table beside her. She began flipping through it. The red-head went back to teasing her client's hair.

I sat on the bench beside Vivie. "And…?"

"And I'm going to change my hair color." She plucked at Grumpy Cat who appeared at that moment to have tears in its eyes, but it was only the vestiges of river water. "And I need new shoes." She looked down at her knee-high gladiators. "Maybe boots instead." She patted her thighs. "I guess I can thank having all these holes in my jeans to make it easier for me not to drown. Not so heavy." A sad look over at me. "What do you think?"

"I will support you in whatever you do."

A ruckus at the doorway made me jump to my feet.

A breathless Maria came flying in. "They got him. They put him in the town jail. At the sheriff's office. Know anything about jailbreaks?"

The two gum-chewing ladies gasped at this announcement, as did their clients in the salon chairs. Like a pair of in-sync matadors, the gum-chewing ladies whipped the sheets from around their clients' necks and shook them like they were tempting *el toro* into an attack. Chunks of hair fluttered to the floor, reminding me of the poop-covered feather that had landed on Vivie's hair at the beginning of this whole avoidable mare's nest.

"I read *Escape from Alcatraz* last year," offered Vivie, unconsciously letting her magazine slip from her lap to the floor. "Saw the movie, too. It was on TV."

"Stay with us, Vivikins."

"It won't be anything quite as complicated as that, sweetie," Maria assured her. What Maria then said to me was as far from assuring as anything could be: "Either way, we have to be quick. Those men are desperate for excitement."

As though someone had just announced a food stamp giveaway, the ladies' clients were out of their salon chairs and into the street in front of Hair Today Hair Tomorrow, and this Olympic-like dash without even a glance in a mirror at their new coifs. The redheaded lady was approaching us while, behind her—wad of pink bubble gum clinging to a back molar—the blonde was folding their matador capes by rote as she watched the goings-on at the shop's seating area: us.

The redhead slipped one arm around my shoulders and the other around Maria's then guided our bodies inwards to form a huddle over Vivie. After a cursory glance out the window onto the street, she said, "Let me guess. It's Hiram, isn't it? Up to his old tricks."

Maria, Vivie and I nodded.

"I can help you with that. But we have to get you gals cleaned up. Disguised. Especially you, young lady. What the hell is that thing on your shirt front anyway?"

"Grumpy Cat."

"That's the first thing we're going to get rid of." The redhead pulled up one of Vivie's exposed bra straps high enough that when she let it snap back into place, Vivie cringed. "Get you into some decent clothes." Her fingers dove deep into Vivie's purple hair like she owned it. "Then we'll deal with this godawful sight."

The blonde, who had even bigger hair than the redhead, inserted herself into our huddle and cut in, "Poor wee thing. What was it attacked you?" She patted Vivie's knee. "Tore up your slacks like that?"

"That's the style, Shirley. Doesn't make it anywhere nice or fashionable, but it's the style."

"I'm glad I left the Earth Plane when I did if it came to this."

Shirley shook her head and not a hair on it moved. "From what I understand, all you other gals need to do is make a wish or something? Is that how it works?"

I was in the midst of opening my mouth to reply 'T would be grand, wouldn't it? when a breathless Muriel arrived in the doorway, having divested herself of her flowing robe and now sporting a lovely silver and blue dress that would fit into any situation from garden party to PTA meeting. Its sequined bodice glittered in the low lights of the salon.

"Like this, you mean?" Muriel fluttered her fingers at me like George had done to transform Vivie's albatross of a purse into a knock-off Louis Vuitton, and Maria and I were suddenly normal, everyday townsladies.

As though this was as normal a thing as seeing a robin yank a worm out of the ground and fly off with it to feed its young, Shirley and the redhead, whose name I later learned was Bonnie, each took one of Vivie's elbows and raised her from her seat on the bench. "We like to do it the hard way. Come along with us," said the redhead. "We have a special room in the back where we perform miracles, too."

Shirley giggled. "It's true. You'll see."

And off they went.

I looked down at myself and although the dress was quite nice, I'd had a special liking for my tie-dyed T-shirt and love beads and I told Muriel so. "That outfit was a gift."

"You know yourself, Sandra, that's what Comfort-Land is all about. Getting rid of our attachments. Maybe it's your fault Vivie and Eduardo ended up back here. Eh?"

"Don't start with me, Muriel. Guilt-Land is still two stops away. And I don't want you pulling this nonsense on me when we get *there*, either."

Muriel ignored this. "Whatever. How about you, Maria? You have quite a challenge ahead of you. Getting Eduardo out of here a third time will be no easy feat."

There was no need for Maria to comment on Muriel's words, the tears welling in her eyes said it all.

Twenty-six

<u>Comfort-Land</u>

WHEN SHE CAME OUT OF that back room of Hair Today Hair To-morrow, I would not have recognized Vivie in a hundred years. I mean, she was beautiful in any light and in any get-up, but with her being scrubbed down to who she really was, she was absolutely stunning, and her grin told me she thought so, too.

"Do you think he'll still like me?" It was a typical teenage girl question, but I sensed a mischievous element in it.

As I guided her out of Hair Today Hair Tomorrow into the street, I said, "If he likes you only for what you look like—"

With a newfound confidence, Vivie interrupted me. "… he's not worth the powder to blow him to Limbo."

I didn't have to ask where she'd heard that.

"Bonnie said even though we are led to believe we dress and fix ourselves up for guys, we actually dress and fix ourselves up for other women. She said it's not any other woman's business what we wear or what we look like. It's our own business. It's a marketing scheme. That's what she said. Marketing. She called it 'moneygrubbing marketing' but with extra words in there that I don't want to say."

I could only imagine.

Vivie flipped her now-brunette hair back. "Did you know

that, Susan?"

"As a matter of fact, I did not."

I felt a tap on my shoulder. It was Maria. "Did I just hear what I think I heard?"

Muriel put her two cents worth in with, "You mean to tell me you didn't know this already?"

Maria now, once more defending me by deflection against Muriel's blows, said, "We're almost there. It's right here."

We ducked into a narrow alley, but Vivie hung back at the entrance to peer out into the street. "Where did Bonnie and Shirley go? I thought they were right behind us."

"What do you mean?" Maria backtracked to where Vivie was, pushed her away from the alley's entrance and cautiously bent forward to look out.

Not to be deterred, Vivie jostled her way back to look out from between the alley wall and Maria.

"They're not there?" I asked, moving in on the other side of Maria.

From behind us came a harsh whisper that conjured a tiny squeal from Vivie and gasps from Maria and me. "This way. Down here."

I don't think I have to remind you what happened the last time Vivie and I were in an alley. But what choice did we have? We followed the ladies. At least we weren't dealing with trap doors and vicious trees.

The sun had come up, so traipsing through the narrow alleys of Comfort-Land on the heels of two bubble-gum-chewing sixty-year-old hair stylists we had just met wasn't quite as frightening as it could have been. Maria showed no sign of distrust toward these ladies but I'm sure that's only because she knew they held a possible key to the rescue of her Charge, Eduardo. Muriel, as usual, was unreadable. Vivie was silent, stern.

The redhead, Bonnie, stopped walking. Do alleys have forks in the road? If they do, we had come to one. One led onto another turn, mostly likely onto another street by the volume of light that slanted in. The other led directly onto a street.

"We have two ways of doing this," she said. "The easy way might or might not work. The hard way most likely will."

"Fill us in," I said.

Bonnie pointed to the street. "We can go that way and just plain old walk into the jail and demand the release of your boyfriend."

"Ooh, boyfriend. That is *so* adorable!" Shirley threw her arms around Vivie and hugged her fiercely.

Vivie pushed her away. "You're worse than Maria with your hugs. You're like a boa constrictor with arms."

Even Muriel laughed at that.

"And he's not my boyfriend."

To break the tension, I jokingly recommended we smuggle in a cake to Eduardo. "With a file in it."

"We'll need a bottle of alcohol for Hiram for sure," said Bonnie, and this wasn't merely a suggestion. "He will be in the sheriff's office." With an air of authority, Bonnie took the way that led directly to the street.

Maria shrugged. Shirley said, "Worth a try." Vivie grabbed my arm to pull me along and off we all went.

This alley came out onto a street I was unfamiliar with. To my left, an overhead sign sported three white cartoon ghosts on a black background. Each ghost had a speech bubble with the word "boo" in it. "Let me guess. Boos stands for booze?"

No one responded so I assumed I was right with my guess. Like I said, the clever names of shops in Comfort-Land were more creepy than comical to me. What kind of mind made these names up? Or did I want to know?

On a signal from Bonnie, Shirley headed into Boos.

"We'll wait here." With both forearms raised against any further forward motion, Bonnie kept the rest of us from following Shirley into the store. "You're under age," she told Vivie. "And besides…"

Maria giggled.

"What?"

Maria took my arm to turn me in the other direction where another overhead sign actually made me cringe.

AYE'S PIE

"Yes. Aye's Pie is a bakery run by a Scot."

"Not a pirate?"

"He's also a Councilman. Politicians and pirates. Same thing." I think Maria recognized my discomfort as being not too far flung from her own. "The ayes have it?" She looped her arm through my elbow. "Anyway, we are going cake shopping."

"The file thing. That was a joke."

"I know," Maria said as she pulled me along. "A good one that held an excellent idea that we simply *must* follow through with."

I called back to Muriel, pointing at Vivie who had her nose pressed to the window of Boos. "Keep an eye on her for me, please?"

Twenty-seven

<u>Comfort-Land</u>

INSIDE AYE'S PIE, A STORE-WIDE counter cut the room in half, its glass front gleaming in the overhead lights. The rear wall was covered with photographs and posters of every cake, pie, muffin, scone, croissant, bagel and cookie imaginable, many of which were displayed in real life on shelves inside the counter. On my side of the room were framed certificates and awards; and on Maria's side sat three tiny wrought-iron tables with two wrought-iron chairs each. It was quite a pleasant atmosphere, to tell you the truth. But then…

Through a beaded curtain behind the counter came none other than George.

"Seriously?"

"What are you doing here?" This was a side I had not seen of Maria. She was always so upbeat, joking, pleasant and here she had actually growled at George. Was the pressure getting to her? "I can't imagine it's work." She sounded downright nasty.

George made his typical palms-in-the-air shrug. "Hey, be nice."

"I asked you what you're doing here."

"What else? Working."

I didn't dignify that with a laugh, but Maria did and not

her usual guffaw.

She continued her interrogation of George. "Where's Ian?"

"Not that it's any of your business, but he's moved on to finer things, finer places. How can I help you ladies?"

"Is this the only cake shop in town?" I stepped in now, fully knowing the answer would be yes, but I had to ask.

"This is it, ladies." George's grin had to be the most annoying in all of creation. "I don't imagine you two just stumbled in here thinking it was a shoe store. I mean, there's a big old pie on the front window." His laugh was just as annoying as his hideous grin.

Maria turned her back to him and whispered, "Looks like we don't have much choice. Do you want to ask him, or must I?"

"Eduardo is your Charge." I tried, but couldn't prevent myself from smiling at her. "Sorry. This is serious, I know. It's just nerves. Sorry."

Maria spun around to face George. "We need a cake."

"Looks like y'all came to the right place."

Oh, ha ha.

"A big one. Triple layer. Chocolate. Can you even bake a cake?"

"I don't have to. I have staff."

Of course, George had staff.

"Big triple layer chocolate cake." All business-like, George scribbled this on a small Aye's-Pie-logo-sporting notepad on the countertop. "Anything else, ma'am?"

"Go ahead," I told Maria. "Tell him."

"We're in kind of a hurry so do you have one ready?"

"I'm sure we do." George turned toward the beaded curtain, then back to us. "Hang on a sec. If you don't mind." He disappeared through the beads.

I heard voices: George's, a female voice and a male voice. Then George was back behind the counter.

"It's not frosted yet. That'll take a few minutes. Care to be seated?"

Maria elbowed me in the ribs as she said, "Actually, can you hold off on the frosting for a jiffy? We have to go do something."

George parted the bead curtains again to call into the room behind. "Hold on a minute with that order."

"Where's the nearest hardware store?"

"Hardware store, eh?" George's eyes moved back and forth from mine to Maria's. I swear he could read our minds. He stretched out his right arm, pointed. "Three doors over." Yes, I'm almost positive George could read minds because he said, with a knowing look on his face, "It's run by a gal." A dramatic pause. "You're gonna love it. It's called The Wench's Wrenches."

I shook my head as my eyes rolled upwards.

"Has a bit of a ring to it, doesn't it?"

Maria grabbed my arm, and none too gently, either. "Let's go." And she hauled me out onto the street toward The Wench's Wrenches.

I couldn't conceal my surprise. "You are seriously going to put a file in that cake?"

"I am."

In no time we were once again inside Aye's Pie and Maria was holding a file out to George. "I can't believe it. I can't believe it. You ladies are something else. I love it."

File in hand, he pushed through the bead curtain and hollered to his staff, "You're not going to believe this."

I heard muttering, stifled laughter then a rattle of the bead curtains as George returned with a mug of coffee in each hand.

"Sit, sit. It won't be long. Might as well enjoy a coffee while you wait."

Twenty-eight

<u>Comfort-Land</u>

Vivie, Muriel, Shirley and Bonnie were waiting for us two doors over when we walked out of Aye's Pie with our file in a cake in a box.

"Took you long enough!" Vivie snapped. "Where's the jail? We have to go *now*!"

Bonnie shot me an I'm-impressed eyebrow then led us toward the alley we had recently exited. "This way."

Vivie didn't bother waiting for me or my approval, she took off after Bonnie. Maria was next, then me, then the blonde, Shirley. As usual, Muriel tagged along at the rear of the procession.

We ended up at the alley crossroads and took the one with the sunshine flooding in. This led to a back street and a sheriff's office right out of the old western movie, *High Noon*, but minus Gary Cooper as Will Kane.

Before I could stop her, Vivie rushed ahead, leaping onto the wooden sidewalk and was about to burst into the sheriff's office when Bonnie, a lot more lithe for her age than I would have imagined, stopped her.

"Diplomacy, my dear. Diplomacy goes with deceit like ketchup goes with fries. Let the cake bearers go in first and only then—but quickly—enter with the bottle we got from Boos."

Vivie nodded reluctant agreement with Bonnie and stepped away from the door to let me pass. On the way by, I heard Bonnie instruct: "Show him what we want to hide from him first, then distract with what he can't resist."

Methinks Bonnie was one smart cookie. A cookie that bore watching? Had she been baked at Aye's Pie by George?

I entered, and sure enough, Hiram was standing behind the sheriff's desk, just now tucking a carving knife away in his pocket. He leaned forward to set a wooden name plate on the desk in front of him:

Shuruf Hirum

"Hi there," I said, smiling my best smile and hoping it looked a lot more sincere than it felt. "I'm Susan and I'm here to bring a CARE package to the prisoner?"

Hiram scraped his ornate desk chair closer to the desk. He sat, placing the outside edges of his wrists, elbows-wide, on the desk. He puffed out his chest. "A *what* package?"

"Oh," cut in Maria. "It means we care. About the prisoner. You know. A second-last meal type thing."

"I don't understand a word you're saying. And speaking of types of things, *that* is not allowed back in the prisoner area under any circum—Oh, what's this?" His eyes jumped from the cake box to the doorway where Vivie stood waggling a wine bottle above her head.

"This is to comfort him in his last hours. Perhaps…" She let her arms, and the bottle, slump, hung her head and tilted it to one side, lowering her gaze to the floor at the bottom of the desk.

I stifled a laugh. *Well, done, Vivie, but don't overdo it.*

"Perhaps to reduce the anxiety of being incarcerated in so ignoble an edifice."

"Don't understand a dang word coming out of your mouth, neither. But you listen to me, girlie. That has to be tested. Give it here."

"But—"

"No ifs, ands or buts about it. Hand it over."

With feigned reluctance, Vivie gave the bottle to Hiram.

I hoped my sigh of relief wasn't as loud as Maria's beside me.

"It has to be tested." Hiram's big hand went immediately to the cap but paused before he touched it. "This has been opened!"

"Oh dear. That's awful." Vivie batted her eyelashes. *This kid was good.* "How did that happen?"

"Where did it come from?"

"Boos," Bonnie offered. "Where else?" *Easy, Bonnie. Easy.*

A satisfied grin bordering on that of George's best, spread across Hiram's face. His gaze was full on with the youngest member of our group, believing—surprise, surprise—that he could intimidate her. "Listen, girlie. You can't fool an old dog with new tricks." He unscrewed the cap and tipped the bottle toward his mouth, lips eager for the tasting. "We'll just see what's really in here. Won't we?"

I will never be able to describe the look on Hiram's face when he got that first taste into his mouth.

"It's rum!"

"Oh dear. They made a mistake. I'd best return it then. Give it to me."

"No way."

"It's not for you. It's for the prisoner."

"No way."

"Well then. I suppose you want the cake too then."

"No way." Hiram sipped again. "It's the best of the best of the best rum I've ever tasted."

Maria took this opportunity to snatch the keys from a hook

on the wall near the back room door and took off with the cake.

As Hiram glugged down about a quarter of the bottle, I heard the jarring squeak of an iron cell door opening down the hall where Maria had gone. Mutterings. A click of iron on iron as, I assumed, the cell door was shut again.

Wearing a subdued smile, and arms down at her sides, Maria appeared at the doorway. It wasn't her usual thumb's up, but I know we all spotted the thumb that extended from her skirt at mid-thigh level.

"We'll be off, then," she said sweetly to Hiram.

"Best rum I ever had. Best." Was it my imagination or was he already slurring?

Bonnie took charge again. "Let's go ladies. We've wasted enough of Sheriff Hiram's time. Thank you, Hiram. Say thank you to Sheriff Hiram, ladies."

We muttered a variety of thank you, thanks, 'preciate your kindness, and off we went into the street and into the alley's mouth once more.

"We did it!" I said and Vivie and I high-fived each other.

"Not to be a Debbie Downer or anything," Bonnie said with a concerned frown, "but now for the hard part."

"I thought that was the hard part."

"Getting Hiram to drink rum is never hard."

"So what's the problem with the 'easy' way then?"

"He gets nasty. He's liable to hang your friend even before the trial."

"Trial?"

"Trial?"

"For what?"

I can't remember who said what during all this worry over Eduardo, but I know Bonnie said, "We have to hope he drinks enough to go unconscious first."

"What did you put in the rum?" I asked.

"Nothing. It's Jamaican. That particular rum is 169 proof. That's almost eighty-five percent alcohol."

"And?"

"It's practically an anesthetic and if he drinks it like its regular old 80 proof, forty percent, it won't take long."

"Long?"

"For him to pass out."

"Then what?"

Maria said, "Eduardo is filing the window bars on his cell—in case."

"In case?"

"In case Hiram doesn't pass out and we have to use the window. See… I didn't lock the cell door." She giggled. Maria was definitely relaxing back into her old self. "So if—or, let's be *positive* about this and say *when*—Hiram passes out, it will be 'easy' again. Eduardo will simply walk out of his cell and out the front door."

"Um. Excuse me." I'd never seen such a worried look on Vivie's face. "What if the rest of the mob comes to see Hiram?" She pointed to the street.

Sure enough, heading toward the sheriff's office was the mob with Hoe Man in the lead. They weren't carrying shovels or hoes or torches this time, but we still had to stop them. But how?

As we exited the alley, I saw they were all wearing suits of a sort and most of them also sported ties.

Bonnie pushed her way in front of them.

"So, where are you lads off to all gussied up? It's not even Saturday night."

Hoe Man spoke up. "Hello there. We noticed you gals coming out of the sheriff's office. You signed up for jury duty, too? Where you going now then? Trial's starting…" He pulled a pocket watch out of his waist band, squinted at it, tucked it away. "Right about now."

"RIGHT ABOUT—?" Vivie clamped a hand over her own mouth. She blinked twice, then she slipped into butter-wouldn't-melt-in-her-mouth mode. "Why, yes. But unfortunately, there's been a change of venue for the actual trial. We ladies are just going to freshen up first."

One of the men leaned forward to ask Hoe Man "What in hang is a ven-you?"

"And…" Vivie's performance was Golden Globe worthy. "Y'all have to go sahn up again at th'other end of tah-own."

"Where we picked that lad up?" asked Hoe Man.

"No, no, silly. At th'other end of town."

"But there's nothing there," said another of Hoe Man's cohorts.

"Exactly why." Vivie's voice lowered. "There's nobody there to see you. This is all very secret because of the nature of that boy's charges. Understand?"

I could tell they didn't understand anything whatsoever, but they all nodded agreement anyway. Nobody wanted to get shown up as stupid in that crowd. Good way to get yourself hanged.

Raising his arm as though to lead a cavalry unit into battle, Hoe Man said, "Let's go men. We have a civic duty to perform."

And off they went like a drove of sheep.

The coast might be clear enough now to spring Eduardo from the sheriff's jail and get away into Fear-Land before anyone noticed he was gone.

Vivie took off so fast, even Maria had to run to catch up.

Twenty-nine

Comfort-Land

EDUARDO, ALONG WITH MURIEL—NOW BACK in her robe—had been hiding in the shadow of the sheriff's office and had caught the entire exchange between the mob and our group.

"Sheriff Hiram is blessedly unconscious," Eduardo told us. "I could hear him snoring so I decided it would be safe to attempt an escape."

Vivie hugged him.

"It was tense for a moment when one of that mob turned to look at me on their way by." He smiled down at Muriel. "But this lovely lady here distracted him with a flick of her skirt. Actually, with a deft change of costume from blue sequined dress back to robe."

That robe was better than a first responder's vehicle, a hiker's backpack, Linda's pockets and Vivie's purse combined.

"Let's get a move on," I said.

A mutter of agreement thrummed through the group.

Bonnie and Shirley, in turn, hugged me, Vivie, Maria, Eduardo and Muriel.

While Shirley was hugging Vivie, I overheard a whisper: "No wonder you wanted to save him from hanging."

"We'd best be getting back to Hair Today Hair Tomorrow,"

Bonnie said. "I wish you the best of luck on your journey. All of you."

"Me too," added Shirley. Then she winked at me. "Break a wing, eh?"

"What?"

But they were gone into the shadows.

"Where next?" Maria asked, not having seen the exchange between Shirley and me, then before I could mention it to anyone, Vivie and Eduardo moved away together, distracting me from the question.

"What's the name of the next section we have to deal with?" Vivie asked no one in particular.

"You aren't *afraid* to ask?" Maria laughed. "You should be *very* afraid." Her familiar guffaw warmed my heart even though I was terrified. A bit of comedy relief never hurt anybody.

Vivie either didn't hear Maria or chose not to. She had most likely been thinking out loud as she was more intent on getting Eduardo free of Comfort-Land than anything else. Good.

"I'm pretty sure it's called Fear-Land," I supplied. "And that's not the least bit funny, Maria."

"'Tis so."

"'T isn't."

"Is there a boat shop close by?" asked Eduardo.

"What for?" asked Maria.

"We have to get across that… that river, do we not?"

"It will have to be a much better boat than the last one," Vivie said. "And once again, I'm sorry I tipped it over, but…"

"We all have fears," I said. "For your sake, Vivie, we'll check for eight-legged critters before we climb into any boat. And we'll make it a sturdier one, too."

"No need." A guffaw from Maria.

"What?"

"There's a *bridge*."

Thirty

Fear-Land

Without incident or pursuers, we crossed the bridge and made our way to a wide roadway and were about to settle in for the night when Muriel announced she had errands to run. Since she had preceded the word "errands" with an "uh," I had to assume she was fibbing. Isn't it strange how the word "fib" doesn't feel quite so much like a lie?

When I say "settle in," that's another deception of sorts. We had no camping gear, no heavy sweaters, not even an umbrella, and we were planning to spend the night sleeping on the ground in a grove of trees in Fear-Land.

We started out with the best of intentions but ended up taking turns sleeping. There was just something about the place.

The next morning, with Eduardo leading the way, we learned that Fear-Land was a forest whose paths were clear of large roots and rocks as they led upwards. Upwards was good. We would be able to see more from a higher elevation if the trees continued to clear out at intervals like they were already doing. Fear-Land wasn't about spiders and snakes and packs of starving-but-still-strong-enough-to-take-you-down wild-dog packs or bathtubs full of alligators. Fear-Land was… To be honest? Fear-Land was the equivalent of being in one of those really good old horror movies in which the main character—almost always a female in my day—decides to go upstairs instead of booting it out the back door to the garage where the car is, keys and all, and getting away safe. No. Fear-Land was going up those endless flights of stairs all alone and in the dark except for a short fluttering candle in your shaking hand—and there's always a breeze coming from somewhere that threatens to distinguish it—in a creepy old house out in the bush while the audience screams, unheard, like a Guide's voice sometimes: "DON'T GO UP THERE!"

"I have this feeling I'm missing something walking through here," Eduardo called back to Maria who was behind me. "This is not exactly a jungle, but it is not *not* a jungle, either. It is difficult to explain, but I have never done this sort of thing without a machete. Sometimes one in each hand and always with friends carrying machetes, too."

"We're friends."

"You have no machetes."

"True. Do you really believe we need them here? This is a lovely quiet forest. I hear nothing moving around. No chipmunks calling out alarms. No birds singing."

"That is what I am saying."

Maria moved ahead of me. "How are you feeling about that?" I'd never heard Maria play amateur psychologist before. Was she doing it for Eduardo's sake? Or her own?

"I feel strange. Something is being triggered in me, but I do not know how to describe it."

"He's got a point there," I interjected. "It's a little *too* quiet, don't you think?"

"Nah. Don't be silly, Susan. They're responding to us being here. That's all."

"… to *our* being here."

"Huh?"

"Maybe it's the fight or flight response?" suggested Vivie to Eduardo. As she grasped his hand, they increased the gap between themselves and Maria and me.

"The gerund takes the possessive." Even before this was out of my mouth, I knew how lame I must have sounded at a time like this.

"The what?"

"Pure instinct," Vivie told Eduardo.

I muttered agreement to veer attention away from gerunds. I was getting annoyed with my nerdiness.

"It's basic in us," she told him. "The most basic fear is the fear of falling. We're born with that. The next is the fear of loud noises. We're born with that one, too. So are animals. The other fears are learned from experience or from…" She laughed. "Or from early childhood parental lectures about alligators in bath-tubs and crocs in rivers."

Eduardo smiled down at her.

Maria slowed down enough to elbow me in the ribs. My side probably looked like it was sprouting polka dots. "A fountain of info, isn't she? I don't see anything to fall off and as far as loud noises go, we're dealing with the opposite, I'd say."

"Writers tend to be. And watch it with the elbow, would you?"

"To be what?"

"Fountains of information."

I never like it when Maria goes all serious. It was almost like she was as half frightened to death as I was.

"So how come *you* didn't know this about inborn fears, *Petunia?*"

"I knew. I figured she might as well get the glory for pro-viding those gems."

A guffaw from Maria. "Liar."

"Fibber. I prefer the word fibber." I dropped my voice. "And don't call me Petunia around her. I don't want her to think about that. She's got enough on her mind."

A whisper: "You realize we have to split the team up before we reach the border, don't you?"

"Why? I was hoping we could keep them together for as long as possible. Fears are greatly reduced with the support of friends." I glanced around the forest. Yes. Eduardo was right. It was too quiet.

"That's why we have to split them up."

A sigh came unbidden from deep down inside me.

"Having support does not eliminate the fear."

How well I was aware of *that* right about now! I nodded.

"And you'll have to shut up and stand back, too, you know." I knew.

"I have to do the same thing for Eduardo."

"Yes, you do. When?"

"What say we get it over with now?"

I always liked to get unpleasant things over with, too, so I was about to agree with her when Eduardo called back: "Maybe this is why?"

"Why what?" I hurried to catch up to them.

Maria shot ahead, of course, and by the time I got there, was already bent down looking into what I can only describe as the entrance to a tunnel made of overhanging tree branches. At least they weren't mesquite trees.

"Look," Vivie said. "There's breadcrumbs on the pathway."

I'll take that back. Mesquite trees would have been better.

Eduardo seemed to drift off into a memory. "*Podemos ir a rescatar a Hansel y Gretel?*" At Vivie's frown, he apologized. "Have you ever heard of the story of Hansel and Gretel? Maybe we can rescue them."

"Many times." Vivie smiled. "And that's exactly why I'm not going anywhere *near* breadcrumbs in a forest."

Maria and I obviously found this equally amusing. We chuckled in unison as we walked past our Charges to continue along the path we had originally agreed upon.

"Come on. Let us go see what is in there." Eduardo pulled a protesting Vivie along with him and they disappeared into the narrow tunnel.

"Toad poop."

And off we all went to follow a trail of breadcrumbs into a Fear-Land forest.

Thirty-one

Fear-Land

RIGHT AROUND THE TIME MY neck was about to fuse in its pre-human, four-on-the-floor position from crawling through the narrow corridor of overhanging trees, we emerged into a larger passageway. I was beyond relieved to once again stand up straight. I flipped my head back and forth like a boxer about to enter the ring. Believe me, though, I wasn't dancing on the balls of my feet and flapping my boxing gloves down at thigh level.

"You guys all right? I'm certainly not."

But once again, out of hearing or caring, Eduardo had disappeared around a turn in the path ahead with Vivie in tow and Maria close behind.

"Wait for me."

I came around that turn in the path and almost knocked over all three of them. They had stopped dead.

That's it. I've lost my mind.

I kid you not. There stood either a house made of actual gingerbread and cookies and chocolate or there had been some extremely talented yet demented designer at work in this section. To maintain my sanity, which, I admit, was slipping, I opted for the latter.

But then, Eduardo, still dragging Vivie along with him,

approached the house and broke a piece off a chocolate-colored windowsill. Dust drifted into the unkempt flower bed below the window. He offered the piece to Vivie first. She would have no part of it.

Good girl.

Eduardo opened his mouth with his lips spread apart and inserted the narrowest end of the windowsill chip. His teeth closed on it. The end broke off in his mouth. He closed his lips and like a wine taster, wiggled his jaw this way and that. He chewed briefly, swallowed.

"Not as good as my grandmother's *dulce de chocolate*, chocolate fudge, but nothing is as good as my grandmother's. Still, it is *delicioso*." He held out the remains of the windowsill chip to Vivie. "Try it. It is very good."

With the tips of her index finger and thumb, Vivie took it from him, I think to be polite more than anything else, and was about to take a bite when I yelled at her.

"Vivie! No. No. Remember what happened to… to… to What's-Her-Name. That Greek girl who ate the pomegranate seeds."

Vivie stopped a millisecond before her teeth made contact with the windowsill chip. "Ah. Yes. I mean no. Here." She handed the windowsill chip back to Eduardo. "And don't eat any more of that! Throw it away!" Then changing her mind once again, she snatched back the piece of windowsill chip she'd rejected and tossed it into the flower bed.

The chip flew from Vivie's hand. It landed with a *poof*. A mushroom cloud formed. Remained.

"MAKE YOURSELF VOMIT!" screamed Maria.

She ran to Eduardo and grabbed his face. "MAKE YOUR-SELF VOMIT!" She forced open his jaws and jammed her index finger down his throat as she repeated the order.

From where I was I could see that it was already too late.

Eduardo's eyelids fluttered. I was reminded of a comment from dear little Sophia about how rolling my eyes was creepy to her. It was creepy. For absolute sure, it was creepy.

Already convulsing, Eduardo crumpled to the flower bed where he thrashed among the dead and dying daisies and begonias. Maria was on her knees beside him almost as fast as he had fallen. "Quick. See if you can find a stick to put in his mouth so he won't bite his tongue."

A quick glance told me that even if there were a stick lying around in this place, I would not put it into the mouth of an attacking zombie much less into Eduardo's. "I don't think much is safe around here, Maria. We have to let it work its own course."

Beside me, Vivie was in tears. "Flip him over on his stomach. Maybe it will come up and out."

It took all three of us, but we managed to get Eduardo onto his stomach over a small decorative boulder. Sure enough, one convulsion later, up came something foamy. When it oozed itself onto the ground, it *poofed* and became a cluster of mushroom clouds.

"Wipe his mouth!" But before Vivie could hold out her new skirt from Hair Today Hair Tomorrow to do the deed, Maria was wiping off her own skirt on the jagged grass.

Eduardo coughed. He groaned.

"Oh, sugar-pie. You OK?"

Eduardo struggled to his feet.

"Eddy?" Vivie caressed the side of his face. "It's me. Flaca."

"Eduardo?" I swear Maria's eyes were as big as Eduardo's. "Hello. It's me. Can you see me? Can you see Vivie? Can you see Susan?"

His eyes went from Vivie to Maria to me. "Who are you people?" Those beautiful eyes of his widened even more. "*What* are you?" He staggered backwards a few steps, shaking his head.

"No." An arm shot out to push us away. "No."

Then like a rabbit with dogs and hunters behind it, he disappeared along the path that led around and behind that horrid little house.

"Rat rears," said Vivie and she took off after him at a dead run.

I wasn't far behind her and neither was Maria.

Thirty-two

Fear-Land

WE DIDN'T SO MUCH CATCH up with Eduardo as it was more like we found him at the side of the path. I think the politically correct euphemism for "passed out" is "sleeping deeply"? No, he was passed out.

The three of us did what we could to rouse him from his self-induced coma but eventually gave up and decided to camp *in situ* for the night. There was no way we could carry this boy. "Dead weight" is a term not wholly reserved for the actually deceased. And no, he wasn't deceased. We checked with a mirror from Vivie's purse. I knew that treasure trove would eventually come in handy.

"The poor boy," Maria whimpered over him. "Maybe we should go back to that house. See if there are any blankets in it. He looks so cold."

"You *are* out of your mind," I said. "I always suspected it, but now I know it's true."

She didn't have a comeback for that one. She was beyond worried. I was too. And Vivie? Vivie was at her wits' end.

After a restless night of taking turns on watch, we were all relieved to see that Eduardo had suddenly and without any notice, sat up, stretched, yawned and resumed being Eduardo.

Vivie and Maria opened their mouths simultaneously but were hushed by Eduardo's raised hand. "I know. I know."

"Are you quite all right, sugar-pie? Any gaps in your memory?" Maria was maintaining her sweet demeanor, but I knew it wasn't about to last for long.

Vivie's aura at head level was a stormy gray swirl. I now understood the origin of the term, steam was coming out of one's ears.

"Well?"

"I am feeling a bit below the weather, but otherwise… Why?"

"It's *under* the weather," Vivie snapped. "You had us scared to death!"

"Don't you EVER, EVER, EVER do anything so STUPID again." Maria's blast of rage blew a gust of energy my way, too.

I resisted the urge to ask Vivie for her mirror so I could check my face for powder burns.

I expected an apologetic bowed head and a kick of pebble from Eduardo, but instead, he straightened his shoulders and his attention strayed to something behind us.

Dare I look?

I looked.

Vivie and Maria turned, too.

No. Please no. I couldn't help myself, I burst out laughing.

The woodsman standing there didn't seem to think his appearance was as funny as I thought it was.

"The woodsman now? Who is doing this? Is it you, Vivie? Are you conjuring all this up in your head like you did with the lynch mob?"

Maria sidled over to me. "Nobody's doing it. Everybody's doing it. This is Fear-Land. Didn't those old fairy tales scare *you* when you were a kid?"

"You mean…?"

"Fairy tales are universal. Every culture has them. Why?"

"I don't know."

"Listen to *her* now, will you? The *writer* finally doesn't know *everything*."

"Um. Excuse me." The woodsman, balancing the biggest ax on his shoulder I'd ever seen, stepped between us. He was tall!

"What?"

"What?"

"Learn this lesson well while you are here," he said. "Learn what fear elicits." He turned away and with perhaps only three or four long strides he was inside the forest. He didn't turn around when he added: "There will be a test. For all of you."

I wasn't expecting this. "A what? When?"

He called out again. "If you learn the lesson here, you'll recognize it there. So pay attention."

I wasn't certain at first that I'd heard right but when Maria guffawed, I knew I had. The woodsman had added something about "Sandra" and "handful."

I turned to Maria. "What's so funny!"

She doubled over.

Thirty-three

Fear-Land

WITH A PROMISE TO MYSELF that I would not be surprised at anything we would encounter along the paths that snaked through
Fear-Land, we forged onward with me in the lead this time. But
silly me had forgotten the admonition never to promise anything
unless one had complete control over all possibilities and even
then…

Ahead on the path, almost hidden in the shadows, appeared
a young woman in combat gear, complete with one of those big
huge guns I think they call AK-47s.

"Have you seen my troop?" she asked. "They went off to
work yesterday and didn't return."

I turned to ask the others. "Have you seen any signs of this
lady's troop?"

Maria and Vivie shook their heads but Eduardo, always Mr.
Gallant, asked, "If you give us a more complete description of
the individuals, we could watch out for them along our way.
Inform them you are looking for them."

Her smile drooped to half-mast leaving one corner up in a
smirk. "I was hoping more along the lines of being able to draft
you people into helping me."

"Oh, really," I said.

"Yes. Really. And who are you who would dare have the effrontery to speak to me in this manner?"

I wouldn't swear to it, but I think her AK-47 shifted slightly from pointing down at a 0-degree angle up to maybe a 5-degree angle.

"We *are* in a bit of a hurry," offered Maria who had moved up beside me by now, attempting to insert herself ahead of Eduardo the Gallant.

The barrel of the AK-47 shifted to 20 degrees. "There are seven of them," she said, her pale face flickering in the shadows thrown by the overhead tree leaves. Her lips were the reddest I'd ever seen. Outside of reality, that is. My imagination found them familiar.

"Do I know you from somewhere? I mean, have we met?"

A semi-laugh, or perhaps more of a plain old *hah*—and a weak one at that—came from those blood-red lips of hers. "Hardly."

Ooh, la-di-dah. "In that case, what makes you think *we* can help *you*?" I didn't add out loud, Or would *want* to.

"What makes *you* think you can't?"

"Excuse me, ma'am!" But before Eduardo could advance on this strange, pale, red-lipped woman with a coal-black dye job that would have made Bonnie and Shirley at Hair Today Hair Tomorrow cringe to the point of tears, Maria pushed him back toward Vivie who was behind me. Maria sidled in behind me, too.

Great. Just put me in the front line, will ya.

I heard Maria whisper. "We have to use diplomacy here. Hush."

"Bring him forward." The AK-47's angle increased to 30 degrees. "He is quite handsome."

A gasp from Vivie.

"You hush, too," I told her behind my hand. "Not one single

word."

"There will be no secrets from me. What did you say to that girl?"

"Uh. I told her she should say 'excuse me' when she burps."

"*Hah.* Bring him here. He has an air of dignity about him. Which, I must say, is lacking in his serv— in his companions."

"You can say that again," I tossed back at Maria.

"Come out from behind there, Sire."

Eduardo stepped out and around ahead of me.

"Well?"

"I am sorry, ma'am. Well what?"

"BOW TO ME!"

Eduardo turned away from her to show us a facial expression that could only mean, This woman is right out of her mind, isn't she? He swung back and bowed from the waist at the young woman.

Maria, Vivie and I plucked the edges of our skirts out, much like Muriel had done at the caldera, what felt like so long ago, and we bounced a curtsy.

"That's better."

"What can we do for you? Um… ma'am," I offered.

"I will speak to your Prince only. Not to his underlings." The AK-47 went back to its 0-degree angle as this strange woman took hold of Eduardo's arm to lead him into the forest. "The path they usually take is this way."

We followed with me in the lead again.

Thirty-four

Fear-Land

Vivie seemed to be the only one who had her wits about her. She came alongside me and asked, "Is it just me? Or does she look alarmingly like Snow White?" Her frown made her eyebrows almost touch in the middle. "I thought Snow White was supposed to be really nice."

"No, it's not just you."

"We never *did* hear what went on with the happily ever after," whispered Maria over our shoulders. "Did we?" She suppressed a giggle.

"Shh," I said. "I don't think we want to rile this gal. She doesn't look all that 'happy,' does she?"

Brushing cobwebs off ourselves, we came out of the trees to a narrow path that led upwards.

"Wait," Vivie told me and reached up to just below the nape of my neck.

"What are you doing back there? No, wait. I don't want to know, do I?"

Vivie came around to the front of me with one palm up. "You're right," she said. "They are a bit adorable in their own way, aren't they?"

I had to bend a bit to see what was walking around on her

hand. Its body was less than a quarter inch long but so brilliantly colored, it made the wee creature almost mesmerizing.

Maria was right there in an instant, too. "Oh. Aw. Look. A peacock spider. They are *so* adorable, aren't they? Is he going to *dance* for us?"

Vivie stepped to the side of the path to deposit the spider on a bush. "There you go, little laddy. Hope you find a wife who's good to you."

A loud *AHEM* from the bad dye job brought us back to our current situation.

"What?" I said. "We're saving lives here."

No, Don't! But she did. She crossed her arms and tapped her foot like Trevor often did, Thumper-the-Rabbit style. "Prince Edward has made the brilliant suggestion that we split up and search from a central core."

I had to turn away so that crazy broad couldn't see my face, but in doing so, I exposed my expression to Vivie and Maria who couldn't stifle their laughter this time.

"What's so amusing?"

"My friends here have absolutely no compassion about another's pain." I reached down to massage my calf, thus hiding my face yet again. "I got a cramp in my leg."

Maria leaned in to whisper, "Did you know that when you fib, your aura goes kind of a pale lime-green color?"

"No I didn't and ask me if I care."

"What's all that jibber-jabber going on there? We have a task to perform. Get over here."

"Yes, ma'am."

I don't know who it was snickered behind me. I suspected it was Maria and I was probably right, but Vivie had been coming into her own so well here, I wouldn't leave her off the list of suspects either.

Eduardo stepped slightly ahead of Ma'am. "I will attempt to

explain how we are going to handle this critically important situation." Well now, look at Eduardo, all prince-like and bossy. "You" (meaning me) "and she" (meaning Vivie) "will go that way." He pointed back the way we had come.

"You think that to be wise, my love?" This was Ma'am, putting her three cents' worth in.

"Oh, yes, my love. I think that to be very wise. This is the only way it will work. Trust me, my love."

I actually felt somewhat sorry for that young woman. How could anyone be that naive as to be lied to by a lover who wasn't all that good an actor?

"And you" (meaning Maria) "and I will go that way." He pointed downhill along a narrow path that led off the one we were currently on. "You two" (meaning me and Vivie) "go now. Go, go, go. Don't be so difficult. Oh, these peasants can be such… such a handful." He winked at me before turning again to the young woman.

It took me a moment before I realized what was going on. I snagged Vivie's arm. "You heard his highness. Let's go. Peasant."

Vivie sputtered something inaudible and I hoped it was as inaudible to "Her Highness" as it was to me. To her credit, Vivie didn't protest further and allowed me to guide her away, back along the path.

As Vivie and I stepped away, I heard "Prince Edward" speaking to the young woman. "We must part again, my love. You carry on with this path, and I shall carry on with that one. Oh, my love. I shall miss you so. Behold, a chaste kiss upon one another's brow as we part, to seal our promise." I heard a *smack, smack.*

"Farewell, my prince, my love."

This is where I should have heard the stereotypical sobbing of unfortunate parting, but I heard nothing from her. Was she playing us, too? Was she perhaps brighter than she appeared to be? Perhaps she'd been forced to stifle her intelligence, had been raised to obey her superiors no matter the circumstances. Perhaps out of the *fear* of repercussions? Poor unfortunate Snow White. Born into nobility but condemned to wander Fear-Land for centuries looking for true love but afraid of it at the same time. Well, maybe some day her real prince would come. Yes?

Thirty-five

<u>Fear-Land</u>

"How far does he want us to go? Are we really supposed to be looking for that girl's troop?"

I didn't quite know how to answer Vivie. Military strategy was not my forte.

"What if she follows him? Gets angry again and…"

"What if we turn around and continue with our original plan?"

"Good idea," said Vivie and she twirled on one foot then with perhaps three times more speed than she had been maintaining *away* from our original plan, she took off.

I had to be quick.

"I'm so afraid for Eduardo."

"He's not your baby."

"I know," she snapped. "I love him."

"You love him."

"Yes. So I'm afraid for him."

"I see." It was all I could do to walk that fast and talk at the same time. I'd have to keep my sentences short if I wanted to maintain my dignity as a Guide. "So… You see him as some helpless little baby? Not the grown man he is?"

"Aren't you afraid for me sometimes? You certainly act

like it."

"Our case is different."

"Different how?" She stopped walking and faced me. Her eyes weren't exactly in slits, but close enough. "Love is love, isn't it?"

Oh, boy. Did I want to get into this right now?

"Isn't it?"

"Well…"

"Humph. She's going to give me the old 'yes and no,' isn't she?" Vivie whirled away again. "They probably went this way." She ducked into an almost hidden pathway. "I think this goes past that awful gingerbread house."

"Did you just say 'humph'?"

Vivie laughed. That was a good sign. "I guess I did. Must be the environment. How do you spell that? H-u-m… f?"

"P-h. H-u-m-p-h. And don't ever use it in any of your writing unless you're writing a—"

"I know. I know. A Gothic romance." She laughed again then reached out to take my hand. "Let's get moving. I want to find him and Maria before that crazy princess catches on to his trick."

We were no more than let's say five hundred feet along the path when, I swear, Vivie jumped an entire foot into the air. I jumped maybe six inches.

We did not jump vertically. No. It was in a horizontal arc off the path to avoid being run down by a rather hairy, old, helmeted man on a tricycle. A two-seater, white tricycle. Picture it.

He didn't exactly screech to a halt, but his tires made a feeble squeak on the moss of the path. He turned his contraption around and came up beside Vivie.

He spoke loudly, as though he were hard of hearing. "Hello, young lass. What, pray tell, are you doing in this neck of the woods?"

Vivie opened her mouth to answer but he didn't give her

a moment.

"Ah. I know. You are seeking a lost love. Yes?"

Vivie opened her mouth again to answer.

"I know where they are."

"Excellent," I said, distinctly enough for a hard of hearing person to understand me. And I even stepped in front of him to allow him to read my lips, if he needed to do that. "Would you mind pointing us in their direction?"

I'm not sure if he merely didn't hear me or he was ignoring me in favor of continuing to natter away at Vivie. He was looking directly at her.

"They went that-away." His chin pointed ahead on the path. "Hop on. I'll take you."

Vivie was in the process of gathering her skirt up so she could throw a modest leg over the seat behind the man's seat when I noticed his jacket's fleece lining.

My hand shot out to prevent her from climbing onto this man's white tricycle.

"Vivie. This guy's wearing a sheepskin jacket."

"So?"

"You say something there, girl? Speak up. My hearing's not the best."

Wait. He couldn't see me. "He can't see me. You know what that means."

"So? He knows where Eddy is. I have to go to Eddy."

"Vivie. No. Don't do this."

She ignored me and climbed on behind the hairy man in the helmet.

"Hang on, girl. Get ready for a bumpy ride."

Oh, dear.

"I like your tricycle. Is there another one near here?" Vivie was one smart girl.

"Eh? What's that you say?"

She repeated her question at an ear-splitting volume.

"Not exactly a tricycle," the man's voice drifted back. "It's motorized. It's back in the bushes where I picked you up. When I found this, I dumped that one in an instant. Right there. I don't really like them new-fangled machines in the first place so never really learned how to work that baby right."

But I knew how to work that baby right. After the movie *The Wild One* came out, all the boys of that generation—the one before me—wanted to rebel like Marlon Brando, so girls (and their parents) got to learn a lot about motorcycles, too, and passed that information on down the line. I found the old dude's cast-off bike easily—it was a motorized trail bike—and I caught up to Vivie and the old dude in the sheepskin jacket. The noise of the motorbike wasn't terribly loud, so I was able to tag close behind them. He didn't even know I was there. Obviously, his hearing was very bad.

I thought nobody could lecture like Trevor, but I was wrong. This guy just wouldn't stop.

"Well let me tell you a thing or two about love, girlie. Women don't appreciate men who aren't princes. When they find out their man isn't a prince after all, they begin to treat them poorly. And yours, girlie, most certainly isn't a real prince. He's pretending to be one to save his own behind."

"Ours, too," Vivie inserted when the old dude took a breath. She said it loudly enough to frighten off any forest creatures if there had been any around, but he didn't react.

I was reminded of a friend of my father who was very hard of hearing and also so ashamed of it, he wouldn't admit it even to himself. Instead, he adopted a habit of non-stop assuming you were interested in everything he was saying. If you asked him a question—even something as common as how are you—he would reply with what he was up to errand-wise that day or had been doing that day or how lovely the weather was or how cold it was. He never asked a single question, either. I think you get the idea. I'm afraid this unfortunate old tricycler was afraid of being mocked for having a disability that most of the world, even animals, eventually dealt with. Parts just wore out.

"You know, of course, that a woman can ruin a man by expecting too much of him. Expecting that he's a prince with an endless source of income that he doesn't have to work to earn. You know what that can do to a man?"

He wasn't expecting an answer but Vivie replied with "No" anyway.

"That can make a man turn to… shall we say… a different path in life. One that might lead him to unsavory practices like going out and stealing it. You know what I mean?"

This time he actually turned his head back toward Vivie, expecting an answer.

"Just nod your head," I whispered.

She nodded. Then shook her head. "I don't know what he means. I don't know what he's talking about."

"Every woman is a princess. At least that's the way we fellows are supposed to treat them. They expect it. They expect to get a card on their birthday. They expect us to remember the day we got married." At this last comment, he nearly lost control of the two-seater tricycle. "Sorry about that, young lady. These old arms aren't as strong as they used to be."

Vivie *hmm*'d a reply.

"Now, where was I? Ah yes." He laughed again. "I'll ask you, what man alive would want to remember the day he lost his freedom and became an organ player's monkey on a chain?"

Vivie *hmm*'d again.

"Not a one, I tell you. Not a one." He slowed his tricycle down to go over a tree root in the trail. "If I didn't come up with a gift on our anniversary, or on her birthday, she would go wild on me. She made me do it. It was her made me do it. I wasn't like that at all until I got involved with the likes of her."

He slowed for another tree root and over we went. We were ascending into a more heavily treed area of the forest and the path was getting rougher and narrower and I didn't like this one bit.

"So I went to a jewelry store that one time, and got her a magnificent gold chain necklace. I have to admit that I liked it a lot, too. She was delighted but then got all serious and angry wondering where I got it from.

"See… I was being prince-like, y'know? Not working. Princes don't work. Princes are rich because… Well, because their… Their families are rich. Nobody in their family ever had to work. She wanted a prince." He snickered. "She got one.

"You should have heard her when the cops came to pick me up and put me in jail. You'd think she wasn't involved in this bit of larceny at all. She even had the unmedicated gall—"

"The unmitigated gall," I muttered. I couldn't help myself. This guy was making me nervous.

"… the unmedicated gall to divorce me when I was in prison."

We went over another tree root.

And stopped.

"That's why, girlie, I can't let you do it to that nice young man of yours. You have to realize he is not in any way a prince and never will be. If I don't stop you, you'll ruin his life. Like she ruined mine." At this, he hopped off the tricycle and pulled a knife out of his sheepskin jacket's inner pocket. "Come with me."

Thirty-six

Fear-Land

AT KNIFE-POINT, THE OLD DUDE forced Vivie into what I can only describe, despite the circumstances, as a darling little cottage in the woods.

I was at first confused that the security bar was on the outside of the door. Once we were inside, my confusion turned into shock.

Yes, there was "Gramma." And what big eyes had *I* at that point. This was not good. Especially since I spotted a hooded red riding cloak draped over a chair in the corner of the living room and a napkin-covered basket on the seat of the chair. I wasn't sure if it was my imagination or not, but I could have sworn there was a cloud of flies swarming over that basket.

"All right, girlie," said the old dude, moving in behind Gramma and holding his knife to her throat. "Do what I say and the old doll won't get hurt."

"Please, please," begged Gramma. "Do what he says."

Her voice was somewhat familiar to me, but I wasn't about to take the chance of accusing her of anything in case I was wrong.

"Put on that riding cloak over there on the chair and then help your grandmother cook me breakfast with what's in that there basket."

I stepped in with the intent of getting the knife away from him. He was elderly and had admitted himself that he wasn't all that strong, but since he wasn't able to see or feel me, I wouldn't be able to do anything physical to him.

He raised the hand with the knife into the air and brought it back to Gramma's neck. "And be quick about it."

"How strong are your lungs, dearie?" Gramma asked Vivie, who was by now holding up the red riding cloak by its shoulders with distaste.

"It's filthy."

"All you have to do is cry 'Help. Wolf' and the woodsman will come save us. It happens all the time."

"What?"

"What?"

"Go to the window and yell 'Help. Wolf.' Do it now."

Vivie shrugged, re-hung the riding cloak on the back of the chair and went to the window. She hauled up the sash and leaned down. "Help. Wolf."

"Oh. No. Much louder than that, dearie."

Vivie called out louder. "Help. Wolf."

Gramma was getting flustered. "Oh, my. He'll never hear you at that volume. He's almost as deaf as this old fool. Holler, dearie. Holler with all your might."

Vivie was always good at following instructions. Once you explained alternatives, that is. She gave it all she had: "HELP! WOLF!"

In no time at all, a great crashing at the door produced the very same woodsman from our previous encounter at the Gingerbread House.

The old dude in the sheepskin jacket put his knife away with a sigh that brought his shoulders nearly down to his navel.

"What am I doing wrong here? I try and try to do it right,

over and over again, but it's always the same thing. This danged woodsman shows up and scares me away. All I'm trying to do is save that young man's sanity."

"Let's go, Jerome." The woodsman ushered the old dude out the door but before closing it, he tossed in the plank that had been across the door to bar it on the outside. "And Gramma? Try to remember, OK?" His voice was gentle, but I detected a great deal of impatience beneath that gentleness. "This thing goes on the INSIDE of the door. Don't let him fool you again. Promise?"

All smiles, Gramma promised. "Cross my heart and—"

"*Don't finish that!*" the woodsman, Vivie and I yelled at her simultaneously.

"Hope to… Oh." A giggle from Gramma. "Thank you, Mr. Woodsman."

"Just try…" A grunt from the woodsman and a shake of his head took him out the door to usher the old dude—sorry, *Jerome*—back to his white two-seater tricycle.

I turned immediately to Gramma. "How do we get out of here?"

"Would you care for some tea," she asked ever so sweetly, all granny-like. "I always have a pot ready for guests."

I'll bet you do. Ain't no way I'm going to be drinking any of it and neither is my Charge. "We do have pressing business to attend to, don't we, my darling daughter?"

I got a "Huh?" from Vivie, then a knowing smile. "Oh, yes, Mother. I'm afraid we are going to be too late." She turned to Gramma. "One must never be too late, must one?"

"Oh, of course, dearie. I understand completely. What you do is carry on along the path you were traveling and then take a right, then a left and you'll be at the border of Fear-Land where it meets both Guilt-Land and Grudge-Land. Life is all about choices, isn't it?" I didn't like Gramma's giggle even one little wee bit.

Thirty-seven

The Border of Fear-Land

Our team—Vivie and I, and Maria and Eduardo—met up again just before we reached the next clearing, which ironically enough, was on the top of a cliff. Well, this was Fear-Land and Fear-Land was doing its duty and hanging on for dear life even at its most-remote edges.

"Fear of falling, y' say."

"That's not funny, Maria."

"I didn't intend it to be funny."

Over to our left, Vivie and Eduardo were wrapped in each other's arms.

"I know. They're going to miss each other."

"They are."

"What is Eduardo's big secret, anyway? Why was it so difficult to get him out of Comfort-Land? And will that affect any of us in any way?"

"I appreciate your help with that. And thanks to your Charge, Eduardo overcame his addiction." Maria smoothed out the back of her skirt and leaned her bottom against a huge boulder behind us. I did the same.

"Love conquers all?"

"Doesn't hurt," she said. "Who was your first love?"

"First and last ergo only."

"Huh? You don't make sense even half the time, Susan."

"It was our second date. In a small town in those days, that made us practically engaged." I didn't laugh when I said this. Neither did Maria. "I have no idea what happened. He was driving. I wasn't paying attention to anything. I was digging around in my purse for a pen." I smiled to myself. "One of the many curses of being a writer is that your pens are always running out of ink. Then I was here and Trevor a.k.a. Pete was complaining that I never listened to him. 'I told you not to get involved with that boy. Don't deny it, I know you heard me.' Can you imagine days upon endless days of listening to Trevor?"

"How long did it take you to get through Comfort-Land?"

"I don't know." I held my left wrist out toward her. "I don't wear a watch."

A guffaw. "Come on, you know what I mean."

"It didn't take all that long, to be honest. Trevor can be a real pain—"

"Don't I know it."

"—but he knows what he's doing. I needed to develop personal discipline."

"Nooo. Not *you*."

Maria was very good at getting people to admit things and I didn't want to talk about being in Comfort-Land the first time. "So then. You're telling me that for Eduardo to have somebody to go all gallant on helped him climb out of his depressed state? Oh. Wait. I'm assuming it was some kind of depression that made him self-medicate? Yes? No?"

"Nice subject switch there, Petunia." Her smile was kind. Even though I wasn't sure about her sometimes, she really was a good and true friend. I was the one with the trust issues. She continued about Eduardo: "Yes *and* no. His depression was very real, I'm not going to take that away from him. But self-medicating yourself for depression using a depressant is about the dumbest thing anybody can ever do."

I looked over at Vivie and Eduardo who were now sitting on a log, holding hands and smiling into each other's eyes. "Do you think he'll be able to manage on his own through Guilt-Land? Without having Vivie to be a hero for? He won't get depressed again and re-start the cycle all over?"

"Only time will tell. Right? What about your gal? How will she handle being separated from Eduardo? Her *Eddy*. Grudge-Land is a very lonely place for those who want to think and feel for themselves. Isolation is difficult."

"Like you said, only time will tell." I rose to my feet and dusted off my butt. "What say we go get this over with?"

Thirty-eight

<u>The Border of Fear-Land</u>

OF COURSE, VIVIE SHED TEARS, and I was sure I saw a glistening in Eduardo's eyes, too. I'm not going to lie, I would miss Maria's company and support and I told her so.

The odds of our running into each other again in the future were excellent, but now was not the time to be contemplating that.

Eduardo and Maria took off through the bush leaving Vivie and me to take the cliff option. Whoopee-do.

Unexpectedly—*not*—there were rappelling ropes hanging off the cliff. And harnesses. Three of them. No, wait. Four. One of them had gotten itself wrapped around a gnarled tree on the far side of the cliff face. Did I mention fear of falling? Did I tell you we were still in the Fear-Land section?

"What now, oh great leader? What do you know about mountain climbing?"

"Only that it's not something I ever wanted to do. There has to be another way." As cautiously as I could, I shuffled to the edge of the cliff and looked down. Nothing but rocks and a few scraggly trees. Was that a—? "Vivie. Come here. Is that a skeleton down there?"

"You're hilarious." She didn't move from her position which

was about ten feet from the lip of the cliff. She crossed her arms.

"OK," I said. "Let's pretend it's just a pile of driftwood."

"There's water down there?"

"Might have been a million years ago but not right now."

"What's down there? Exactly."

"Rocks."

"Rocks."

"And more rocks. They're round and smooth but I would imagine they would hurt just as much as pointy ones to land on."

"There has to be another way down. There *has* to be."

"Come here."

Vivie sighed deeply and eased her way over to stand at my elbow.

Below us, the rappelling ropes hung down like Tarzan movie vines but there were no trees to swing from or to. Not that I would be able to swing from tree to tree on a vine anyway. Not with my upper body strength, or lack of it to be more accurate. "What do you think?"

"*I* think we need to find another way." As she stepped away from me again, she emitted a tiny squeak of surprise.

I whirled.

George. In some kind of uniform.

He made a low sweeping bow as he said, "At your service."

"I'd prefer to fall to my death," I retorted.

"Excellent. That means I get Vivie then." Oh, that annoying grin!

Vivie stepped up to him. "What can you do to help us get below?"

The way he used his index finger to point upwards made me think he was about to either remind us of something by shaking it at us, or to start rhyming off a list, one, two, three… but that wasn't so. Vivie looked up and the smile on her face made me look up, too.

Hovering over the forest was a helicopter with a ladder swinging from an open door. Why hadn't I heard it?

"Trees tend to muffle sound quite a bit," George informed me. I didn't want to think it true, but he seemed to be capable of reading my mind way too well.

The helicopter swung low enough that the ladder was merely a foot off the rocky ground and no longer swinging. I wouldn't call it inviting or any less frightening than… let's say riding bareback on an elephant that has just spotted the proverbial mouse? I reached out for the rung above the one at eye level and settled a foot onto the lowest rope step.

"I'll go first," I told Vivie. "Then you follow. If this thing *is* a trick, it's better for me to learn than you."

As best I could as a first experience with climbing a rope ladder which did begin to swing when I was about half way up it, I made it to the top where one of George's goons helped me in.

The goon then leaned precariously out of the helicopter door to show a thumb's up to George.

There was no pilot.

"Who's driving this thing?"

I received no answer but heard a giggle just before Vivie's head popped up at floor level. She clambered in with the goon's help. "This is really cool."

George came next and headed directly for what I could only call the driver's seat as I knew nothing about the workings of a helicopter. Did they use the same terms as they did for airplanes or for cars?

"Well done, Timmy." He slid himself into the driver's seat and grabbed the helicopter steering thing. "Not bad for somebody who never flew a helicopter before, huh?"

"Who? You or him?"

George's answer was drowned out by the helicopter door's

being slid closed by the goon, Timmy.

"Have yourselves a seat, ladies," George ordered. "And buckle in."

Thirty-nine

Grudge-Land

That I trusted George to get us—by helicopter, no less—out of Fear-Land into Grudge-Land at the bottom of that cliff must show you how afraid I was to tackle mountain climbing. Or… Should that be un-climbing if you're on the way down? Regardless, it wasn't exactly a Little Voice in the back of my head, but it might have been. Either way, a thought popped in: What if somebody (since I would be going into Grudge-Land) had set it up to have a person I disliked—had a grudge against?—be the one to save Vivie and me from a prickly predicament?

The helicopter landed in a beautiful meadow and without a word to us beyond "Keep your heads down until you get clear of the blades, ladies," off George went into the sky with his goon.

"What happened to George?" I asked. "The horribly mean snarky George?"

"I don't know and I don't care. All I want is to get out of this stupid place and get to where I can see Eduardo again."

"What did he tell you?"

"That he's going to Guilt-Land and I'm not. He said I have to go somewhere else. I have to go on ahead, he said. Without him. And he'll be without me, too."

"What else did he tell you?"

"Nothing."

"Nothing?"

"Nothing."

"Your aura just flashed pale lime green, you know."

"So what?"

"Come on. You can at least tell me what you felt when he talked to you about this." There I was, sounding like Maria, the amateur psychologist.

"Are we going to just stand around here? Or are we going to do something?"

I had no clue. I'd never been here before. "Uh. What would you suggest, Vivie?"

Her sigh and eye-roll told me I was close to being someone on her Grudge List. "Let's go this way."

We didn't take the pathway that led through the vast meadow, the pathway edged by some of the most exotic flowers I'd ever seen. No, of course not. That would have been too easy. Too pleasant. Off she went into yet another treed corridor with me as close on her heels as I could manage with the speed she was traveling over those eternal, infernal tree roots and rocks.

Forty

<u>Guilt-Land</u>

SURPRISE, SURPRISE? NOPE. NO SURPRISE at all that my Charge had manipulated me into trusting her to lead the way and there we were in Guilt-Land and I don't even recall feeling like we were going back up to the top of the cliff to get there. Did I feel guilty about that? What do you think?

"Seriously, Vivie?"

"Yeah, seriously. Now let's go find Eduardo."

To slow her down a bit, I got her talking about him and his issues, hoping to draw hers out of herself before we got too far into Guilt-Land, before "things started happening" which, of course, they would. Like I said, I was not the least bit familiar with Guilt-Land so didn't have a clue what to expect. I knew only that I didn't want to be here and Vivie didn't have to be.

For Eduardo, it would be worse because of his depression, his guilt-depression cycle thing. Me? It seemed I had always been angry below decks for the last while before my transition from the Earth Plane, so I was scared to be here. Would I have to deal with something lurking inside me, too?

I think Vivie would be fine. I was one hundred and ten percent sure of that, but she still needed me to, yes, guide her. But how could I guide her when I didn't know what I was doing myself?

I didn't know if I could make it through Guilt-Land. I wasn't sure I could make it through anything, let alone save Vivie, and help Maria with Eduardo. I wasn't strong enough. Let me reword that please: I didn't *believe* I was strong enough. Was Guilt-Land associated with self-esteem? It was feeling like it.

To pass the time—distract myself?—we discussed Eduardo's guilt thing. Yes, I managed to get her talking about him and his issues which were surprisingly familiar to me.

"He says it's like this little cloud floats in unnoticed and definitely unwelcome."

"Could you call it a Guilt Cloud?"

"Something like that. Hey, yeah, Ms. Writer. Good way to put it, Susan."

"I guess maybe he has to work it out before he gets to Grudge-Land? I have never been there so I can't speak from personal experience, but I've heard… You know… I've heard things about that place. That it can be the loneliest place ever."

"But how do *you* feel about being in Guilt-Land? I'm picking up funny vibes from you." Was she mocking me? "As if you'd tell me anyway."

"Not sure."

"Will you be explaining it to me or do I have to figure it out myself? As usual?"

"What do you think?" I know my smile didn't look all that sincere, but I was trying to lighten things up for Vivie. "Let's get through Guilt-Land before we start worrying about future possibilities, OK?"

"You're no fun." My Charge was maturing by the minute, standing up for herself. "By the way, I'm starting to see a haze around you sometimes. It's mostly kind of gray, but once in a while I see a flash of color. Now I just have to figure out what the colors mean. Right?"

"You can see my aura?"

"Ah. So that *is* what I'm seeing then. Cool."

Cool, she says. The last thing I needed was for my Charge to know exactly what I was feeling at all times. She was supposed to trust me.

"I guess this means we're even now."

"What do you mean?"

"You always know when I'm lying. Now I'll know when you're lying." She laughed and it wasn't entirely a kind laugh.

"Fib. Use the word fib."

She laughed again.

"I'm afraid you've been hanging around Maria a little too much. Your sense of humor leaves something to be desired."

"Did I ever tell you I love you?" she giggled as she poked me in the ribs with her elbow.

"Ouch with the elbows, huh? You're turning into a Maria clone for sure." I didn't think this was as funny as Vivie obviously did.

At this, she pointed at an area between my shoulder and my chin. "What does red mean?"

I ignored her question and suggested we pay attention to the rocks and roots along the trail, that I didn't want to add to my current troubles by breaking my neck tripping over a cedar root.

Still giggling, Vivie promised to leave me alone—"for now," she added—and we continued on our way until we exited the tree tunnel into somebody's back yard.

"Any idea where we are, or what this is?"

"Looks like maybe the back of a store or something?" She pointed to the rear of the building at the other side of the yard where boxes and barrels had been piled high.

"Maybe a restaurant? Or grocery store?"

Over to one side of the yard, a path led between this building and what was probably a private house as it was complete with white picket fence. I suppressed a smile as I pointed to it. "Let's go find out."

That Vivie and Eduardo had become close was evident in the speed with which she was able to track him down. In the old days, I would've called it radar, but I guess it's called GPS these days. Or maybe just plain old love? We found them in no time at all in an outdoor market, picking through a display of vegetables.

Maria guffawed when she spotted us and came running to dole out one of her crushing hugs, first to me, then to Vivie.

Eduardo tossed a relieved smile in Vivie's direction and she darted to his side at the vegetable stand.

Maria called out, "Grab a couple extra yams?" She turned to me. "You do like yams, right? Also known as sweet potatoes?"

"Right about now, I'd even eat Brussels sprouts if you were offering them."

"And some Brussels sprouts, too," she laughed in Eduardo's direction.

Eduardo turned up a palm as he called back, "Brussels sprouts don't go with my recipe."

Maria flapped a hand at him. "Just joshing with you, sugar-pie. You know what you're doing, I certainly don't." Turning to me again, she went all serious on me, and demanded to know what Vivie and I were doing there. "I thought you were going on ahead. I was actually getting somewhere with Eduardo and now, I will have to deal with distractions again."

"Would you believe me if I told you it wasn't my idea to come here?"

Maria glanced over at the two love birds who were deep in conversation at the sweet-potato section of the vegetable market. "Come with me," she ordered. "We're staying in a cottage down by the creek. It's a pretty little place. So pretty, in fact, it almost makes me want to stay here forever. So, in a way, I *am* actually happy you showed up. It will urge me to work harder and faster on Eduardo because now I am facing the extra challenge of Vivie's interference."

"Glad to be of service." I was always happy to know that sarcasm didn't show up well in auras.

I had almost forgotten how strong her hand was, and how much faster she could run than Vivie, but when she wrapped her fingers around my upper arm and took off dragging me behind her, it brought it all back, in spades.

"Don't worry. He'll be along shortly. He has a roast chicken in the oven. He's an awesome cook. That's what he did on the other side of The Veil. Till he blew up his restaurant, that is."

"He what?"

"Accidentally. Accidentally. They were installing gas lines on his street and they didn't shut off a valve or something the way they were supposed to."

"That's what brought him here?"

"Um. No. Did anybody ever tell you that you ask too many questions?"

"Who? Me?"

We had reached the rented cottage and Maria was right. It was absolutely lovely and even had lettuce and tomatoes growing in the front yard.

"Nice," I said, as I followed Maria through the foyer into the living room. "You're right. I could see myself wanting to stay in a place like this forever, too." We settled ourselves into a couple of really comfortable chairs.

"So. Start talking, Susan. Your aura is a mess. What's going on?"

"Where do I start?"

"Wherever you want. We have forever, right?" I expected a guffaw. This was Maria, after all, wasn't it? But what I got was a gentle squeeze of her hand on mine and as kind a look as I had ever seen on her face.

"I've never been here but I think I've been here all my life. Both my life before and my life after and my life right now. And I don't like it."

Maria rose from her chair and headed toward the kitchen. I could see the stove from here so knew she was putting water on, probably for tea. A commotion at the door, a Vivie giggle and a deep-voiced unintelligible mutter that prompted another Vivie giggle, told me the shoppers had arrived. My conversation with Maria would have to wait.

Forty-one

Guilt-Land

We were gathered around a small table in the kitchen enjoying a chicken dinner so scrumptious I wondered if we had somehow been transported back to Comfort-Land and I told Eduardo so.

I thought perhaps I had said something wrong because he glanced at Maria, beside him, then across at Vivie, before responding with a grunted "Thank you but that is my late father's recipe. Not mine."

"You *are* very good at cooking, you know," Maria assured him. "When are you ever going to believe that about yourself again? It's important to deal with these things."

"You do not have to nag me about that in front of people. Can't you save it for later?"

Vivie's wide eyes met mine.

Eduardo turned to Vivie. "Sorry, but she really gets to me sometimes. I do not need all that negativity right now." He resumed eating.

Maria pushed aside the remains of the chicken dinner on her plate and rested her knife and fork on the clear space. A slight nudge of the plate with her thumb told us she was finished eating and perhaps ready to launch into a rebuttal.

Vivie followed suit with her plate perhaps preparing to rebut Maria's rebuttal?

Not to be left feeling like an outsider, I did the same with my plate. But with regret, as I wasn't finished with my sweet-potato fries.

Eduardo stopped in mid-chew. "You are actually going to do this. Right here. With everyone listening in."

"It's the only way, sugar-pie."

"What if I do not want to participate?"

"Prove to me you don't."

At this, Eduardo clucked.

Vivie gasped, I assumed, not at his cluck, but at Maria's demand.

"That is impossible," he said, pushing his own plate aside. "One cannot prove a negative."

Maria, her grin half filling her face, glanced over at me. "So now he's going all lawyer on us. Can you help me out here, o fount of knowledge?"

"I agree with Eduardo," I said, much to Vivie's obvious relief.

She leaned into him with a comforting pat on his arm. "See? You don't have to reveal anything you don't want to."

"I'm afraid you misunderstood me, Vivikins. I'm agreeing that one cannot prove a negative."

For that one I got a snort each from Maria and Vivie. Eduardo's face remained passive.

"Eduardo must realize—and I refuse to apologize for talking about him in the third person right now because sometimes that makes things easier…" I dragged my plate back in front of me to pluck out a piece of deep-fried sweet potato which I savored slowly while three sets of eyes glared at me. "… this young man is an unbelievably excellent cook—or should I say chef?" I received nothing but a blank stare into Outer Space from

Eduardo. "So I want to know why he ended up here in Guilt-Land. Did he poison someone? Did a small child choke on a chicken bone or something? And I know about the explosion."

A clamped-shut mouth, slight shake of head and raised eyebrows from Eduardo told me I would have to try another tactic.

I exaggerated the following, as was my way. *Sometimes, Mom. It was my way* sometimes *to exaggerate. Not always. Only when I needed to.* I spoke directly to Maria. "I still think it was my fault that we had that car accident on the way home from the drive-in that night and if he had died instead of me, I don't know what my life would have turned out like. Would it have been a guilt-ridden one? Can you perhaps put a couple of cents' worth in here to help me out, Eduardo? The more you can help me, the more I can help Viv—er, Flaca."

A blast of frustrated air came out from between Eduardo's lips. He shook his head. Paused. "Very well. Get comfortable then."

We did.

Eduardo lifted a sweet-potato fry from his own plate and waved it back and forth. "This. This is what happened." He shook his head again. "I inherited the restaurant from my father after he died. I was only sixteen when he passed. I was expected to take the family restaurant to the heights of success, but I never produced a new idea but this one over the next five years." He waggled the sweet-potato fry again. "In five years. Nothing but a french-fry."

We waited for him to continue.

"You said you know about the explosion."

I nodded.

"What explosion, Eddy? Is she telling the truth? You never told me about any explosion. Is that…? Is that how you…?"

"No. That's not how I died. I died from this." He flicked the sweet-potato fry back onto his plate. "This sweet-potato french-fry concept went over very well with the staff and with the first few customers who tried them. Everybody loved them. I had finally accomplished something."

"Well they *are* delicious if these are the same as the ones you're talking about," said Maria.

Vivie and I mumbled agreement.

"The next day, there was a lineup outside my restaurant for the new fries. We were insanely busy until closing time. We ran out of sweet potatoes three times and I had to send a boy out to get more. I think we depleted every single farmer in the market. The restaurant had made a great deal of money with my idea. I had brought my father's dream to the heights of success. Later that night, because we were all so exhausted, I told everyone to go home. I would shut down and lock up."

"Oh, sugar-pie, you must have been so proud."

"Proud? I was so full of myself, I did not think to shut down the deep fryer when I left that night. Proud? Yes. A terrible error on my part. The deep fryer was old so could have burst into flames at any time overnight, but it did not. I wish it had." Eduardo plucked at something invisible on his pant leg. "My sous chef always arrived half an hour before everyone else to get things started." He looked across at Vivie. "Like turn on the deep fryer. The investigating officer's report says it just so happened he took the cover off it, giving it a breath of oxygen, at the exact same instant someone flipped the switch to that new gas line. All it took was that one mistake by me and *adiós al padre de cinco hijos*. Five children lost their father."

Vivie reached across the cluttered table to grasp Eduardo's hand.

He pulled it away. "No, no, Flaca. I must do this on my own. I cannot have anyone babying me anymore. My *abuela*, my grandmother, did enough of that, and that is what got me into more trouble. There were no charges laid against me, thanks to Abuela's influence on a certain member of the *policía*. I should have gone to prison for what I did. I deserved the worst punishment possible."

"But you didn't do anything." Vivie once again grappled for Eduardo's hand. "I mean, it was the fault of the gas people. And you were tired from such a hard day at work. All of you were. Anybody could have forgotten to turn off the deep fryer. And it wasn't your job."

"I hear what you are saying, Flaca. Part of me agrees with you. Up to a point. I was ready to admit it all and forgive myself. Yes, I was. But then…" He smiled at Maria. "You were right, Maria. I got more out of feeling sorry for myself than I got out of manning up. And my grandmother did nothing to discourage those feelings. I think she encouraged them to make me dependent on her, child-like. She missed my father terribly, crying every day over him. I suppose I was his replacement."

I leaned over to whisper to Vivie. "Maybe that old biker in sheep's clothing was right about princes?"

She lifted her lip at me.

"The insurance covered the loss but what did I do with the money? So stupid." This time, Eduardo reached for Vivie's hand. "I am so ashamed. I partied. I drank heavily. I even took drugs sometimes. I was now the rich boy of the neighborhood so everyone *loved* me. Everyone wanted to party with me. *Hah!* On my nickel, of course."

He ignored Vivie's sympathetic head shake.

"When I ran out of money, I ended up living on the street. Grandmother did her best to berate me, but I did not listen to her terms."

"She wouldn't let you live with her? That's mean."

"No, Flaca. She was right. She said I could live with her only—only—if I quit drinking and taking drugs. She no longer wanted me as a replacement son because I had shamed her too much."

"I still think it's mean. She was still your grandmother."

"On the streets, I did what I wanted, what made me feel… better? No. What I *wanted* to feel like. I wanted to feel sorry for myself so I would have an excuse to drink. I got involved with a gang. When you are alone on the street with no money, there are rules." He shrugged. "You have to eat. I needed my daily intake of alcohol. I sold drugs. To children. Even supplied them, without intending to, to one of my sous chef's children." He released Vivie's hand and slumped back in his chair. "You cannot get any worse than that."

Maria's eyes met mine as she said, "Don't kid yourself. You can get lots worse than that. But I won't go into details because I don't want to scare Susan. She's just a kid." Her laugh, although feigned, was enough to lighten the mood, if only slightly.

"Come on, Maria. This is serious. And I can relate to what he's talking about."

"Now she's going to tell us she sold herself on the streets for drugs? In her small town? Now who's not being serious?"

"You know what I mean. It's not the deed itself, it's the doing of something we *believe* we did wrong. It could be anything. Something that isn't wrong at all. We only think so. Like he said, it's stupid."

"What are you guys talking about?" Vivie was going even more all-mommy-mode on us now. "Don't be mean to him. You should never call anybody stupid."

Eduardo leaned forward again to reach for her hand and to whisper, "Your hair is glowing orange."

Maria and I simultaneously: "What? You can see it, too?"

"Vivie spotted mine earlier."

"No!"

"Yes. She did. Now he can. Looks like neither you nor me

will be getting fired for incompetence any time soon." Despite the seriousness of everything that was going on I allowed myself a laugh and I don't need to tell you that Maria allowed herself a good one.

In fact, Maria leaned up from her chair to offer me a high-five. I accepted.

Vivie and Eduardo had locked eyes, let's amend that to say they had locked rolling eyes, and were stifling grins.

Eduardo turned to me. "Can you give me an example? I mean, if you do something wrong, it is wrong, is it not? Wishing it not to be wrong is wrong in its own right." Eduardo's smile made more than me sigh with relief. "Did I just say that? 'Wrong in its own right'?"

Vivie giggled. It seemed she was feeling better too now that her precious Eduardo was showing signs of relaxing.

"I'll go first," I said. "One day, when I was about fifteen, I got mad at my mother. In the book of rules that Trevor gave me—"

"*Guidelines*, he calls them. *Guidelines*, Susan."

"Yeah, right, guidelines. Sorry, but my automatic thesaurus isn't working right now."

"Good one, Susan."

"Anyway. I was absolutely furious with my mother that day. According to Trevor's… *book*…" Maria returned my smile. "… this happens a lot around the age of fifteen. Who'd a thunk it back then? Certainly not us perfect fifteen-year-olds of the 1960s."

"And?" Eduardo prodded. I understood his impatience.

"I hopped onto my bicycle and tore off down the street as fast as I could pedal. I wasn't paying attention to anything in my peripheral vision so didn't see the squirrel."

"Squirrel," said Vivie. "Squirrel?"

"I ran over it."

"Aw."

"As soon as I realized what had happened, I stopped to look back. What I saw ripped my guts out."

Vivie's eyes met mine. "Go ahead. Say it." Her eyes flicked away from mine to Eduardo's then back to mine.

"I don't know whether it was a boy or a girl I had killed. And it was dead, I know that. But another one ran out and fussed over it. Whether it was the squirrel's mate or its mother or its child I don't know. All I know is, I still feel guilty about it and I don't know if I'll ever get over it."

"Wow," said Vivie.

"I guess it's actually the anger against Mom that I felt—feel—guilty about. I knew I had not hit the squirrel deliberately, so why feel guilty about that? But I was being…" I held up two fingers of each hand for quotation marks, "*bad*, so something in me made a quick substitution."

A trio of scraping chairs told me I needed to rise to my feet as well to accept the compassionate hugs of my team, my friends.

"I understand," Eduardo told me as tears brimmed. "Yes. I was wrong to leave the deep fryer on. Yes. That act contributed to Juan's death. I did not do it to kill him. It was an unfortunate accident caused by me and made worse by the gas line error. The mistake I made was using Juan's death to feel sorry for myself. To sink into me, me, me and only me and my desires. Thank you for sharing your story with me, Susan. With us."

He reached to take Vivie's hand, but she was deep into her purse from which she pulled a packet of tissues. His hand was already out so Eduardo got the first one. Maria and I gladly dabbed our eyes, too.

After Eduardo had wiped his eyes and deposited his used tissue and that of Vivie's into the flip-top garbage can in the kitchen, he turned to Maria. "You were right all along. Imagine.

A french fry turned me to drink."

It was good to hear Eduardo laugh.

He continued. "And although I ended up selling drugs to fifteen-year-old children…" He smiled at me. "Yes, they are still children at that age no matter what *they* might think. I did not actually sell anything to Juan's son, who was, for your information, in his early twenties. He stole from me. My drugs. My money. He is the one who stabbed me to death. I had conveniently forgotten about him until your confession about guilt, and how it can bounce from place to place. What a complex piece of engineering is the human mind, *si*? Juan's son was already hooked at the time Juan died. Perhaps grief was *the son's* excuse for spiraling deeper into drugs, theft and eventually murder? How far would I have sunk, I wonder?"

Maria caressed Eduardo's shoulder. "Do you feel any better about things after telling us all this?"

I swear Eduardo's sigh of relief came all the way from his toes, and yes, I'm exaggerating, but that's the best way to explain it. "Grief has many faces, does it not?"

Vivie took Eduardo's hand. Their eyes exchanged kindness, understanding and love.

"Does this mean we can finally get out of here?" I asked.

My answer came in the form of a loud banging at the front door of the lovely cottage.

Now what?

Eduardo stepped ahead of Vivie and reached out an arm to push me back behind him as well, but I resisted his effort and followed Maria to the door.

Maria opened it.

"Hello, Maria. Hello, Sandra. I trust all is well?"

I staggered back about three feet, selfishly leaving Maria to fend for her own safety alone in the foyer.

Like the Little Teapot, Muriel tipped herself over so she

could see past us. "Ah. I see your Charges are still in one piece. Well done, ladies." She didn't exactly push Maria out of the way, but her entry into the living room left Maria clinging to the foyer door like a limpet on the side of a rock.

I scooted over to my Charge and adjusted myself to be dead center in front of her, between her and Muriel.

Muriel's eyes rapidly took in the details of every corner, upper, lower and beyond, of the room then came back to rest on mine. "Where's my hug?"

Forty-two

<u>Guilt-Land</u>

YES, I HUGGED MURIEL AS did all of us before she commanded that we haul our kitchen chairs into the living room and set them up audience-style.

Funny, I hadn't noticed the black chalkboard on a stand against the living room wall when I first came in, but there it was and there was Muriel with a pointer. A pointer. A teacher's pointer. In her other hand was a piece of chalk.

"I understand you were told to expect a test."

Vivie giggled, Maria laughed out loud, Eduardo showed his palms to the ceiling like George always did, and I said, "Well, yes. But."

"But you thought we were kidding. Is that right, Sandra?"

"I'd like to give *you* a test on the proper way to remember a person's name," I muttered. Then out loud, to be polite, I replied in the affirmative to Muriel's question. "Yes, Miss Muriel."

"That's better. Now. I understand Eduardo has managed to work something out regarding pride, guilt, depression and… you, Susan."

She aimed the pointer at me and it didn't wobble the slightest amount.

"You, Susan, have discovered that being angry at your

mother can cause a lot of problems."

"Well, I have one question, if I may." I didn't like being treated like a little kid in kindergarten.

"Ask away, Sandra."

"Where exactly does the rule come from about anger? I mean, it seems to be quite acceptable to be angry at someone who has done wrong to someone else, or even, on some occasions, to yourself. Where does the rule come from that you're not allowed to be angry with your mother?"

Maria had no hesitation whatsoever in answering me with: "From your mother, of course. Who else?"

She, Vivie and Eduardo laughed.

"Flaca said something about that," Eduardo said. "In a way, at least. Back when we were in Fear-Land? My mind is a little foggy on it because I was still recovering from the effects of eating a windowsill." He chuckled. "She was talking about being born with two basic fears then the rest of them come from experience or…" He smiled at Vivie. "How did you put it? Something about parental lectures on alligators in bathtubs? Do anger issues come from similar sources?"

We all looked to what I would call the "head of the class" where Muriel was standing. The expression on her face could not be determined. Once again, she aimed her steady pointer at me. "Sandra? Would you like to answer that one?"

"Of course not. Getting angry with my mother was a really bad thing to do. Nothing got her madder than that."

Maria burst into laughter. "Did you just hear yourself?"

"That is funny," said Eduardo.

Vivie laughed too. "You were afraid to get mad at your mother because she would get mad at you. How come *she* was allowed and you weren't?"

Why indeed?

I heard squeaking noises coming from the chalkboard.

Muriel was busy drawing little circles—bullets, I think they're called—and writing words beside them.

- anger
- guilt
- feelings of unworthiness

Then she turned to us again. "Connect the dots."

Without thinking—being in this classroom-like situation was unnerving—I rose to my feet to sputter, "They're already connected. I recognize the pattern."

Beside me, Eduardo stood up, too. "She is right. May I say something further?"

"Of course, you may, young man. There's no reason to fear me."

I couldn't hold back my snicker so got a glare for that.

Eduardo continued. "It seems to me we are as blank as that chalkboard was before you wrote on it. And experience, or more likely our parents' experiences, get written onto us, but with indelible ink."

Vivie's applause was not in the least bit insincere.

Maria leaped up from her chair to high-five with Eduardo. "Well said, sugar-pie."

Vivie was on her feet to high-five with Eduardo and Maria, then me.

Muriel whirled to face the chalkboard again and with the end of her robe—her multitasking robe—she rubbed out the dots. "Then disconnect them. You must. When you feel one, don't let it lead to the next one. Class dismissed."

Then Muriel had the foyer door open. "All right, kiddies. Let's get moving. We have somewhere to be."

"I just gotta get my purse."

And out of the lovely little cottage we went. I did not want to think about or even slightly imagine even the itsiest bitsiest bit, what might be ahead of us before we managed to get to Grudge-Land. Muriel was with us now, on our team, so it had to be… Well, I didn't like to speak negatively, ever, but it was probably going to be BAD!

Forty-three

<u>Guilt-Land</u>

WE PASSED THROUGH THE MARKETPLACE without incident, Eduardo pointing out various food items and translating them into Spanish for Vivie, or, in some cases even explaining what they were in the first place, like dragon fruit and manioc.

"That one," he said, indicating what looked like a football with pointy bumps all over it, "is called durian." His nose wrinkled. "In some countries, it is illegal to cut it open in public."

A Vivie giggle, then a question: "Why?"

"It smells like… I am sorry, I do not know the polite word for puke."

"Vomit," provided Vivie. "You can't be serious."

"I am, and it does."

"You know so many things about so many things."

Eduardo kissed her forehead. "All part of my job. How do you say it? No biggie?"

"Aw," said Maria. "Aren't they just the *sweetest* couple *ever*?"

I rolled my eyes.

At this point, we had reached the house with the white picket fence and as we stepped onto the path that ran between it and the building beside it—I still had not been able to figure out what that building was for—I could see the forest from where Vivie and I had entered Guilt-Land. There was something odd about it. Although, when we came in, I hadn't actually turned around to look at it from the angle we were at now. Maybe that fence had been there all along?

I turned to Maria. "Are you seeing what I'm seeing?"

"If you are seeing a high prison fence, then we're seeing the same thing."

"Complete with double rolls of barbed wire on top?"

"I believe it's called razor wire," Muriel offered. "And I believe those three characters up ahead are called prison guards."

Three uniformed hulks, two males and one female, had stepped in to prevent Vivie and Eduardo from proceeding farther. Since these people were not looking at Maria, Muriel or me, I had to assume they were permanent denizens of Guilt-Land and couldn't see us.

The two males crossed their arms in the way some bodybuilders do to make their biceps look bigger. The female stepped forward and said, "Visiting hours are over. Time for your friend to leave."

Maria and I exchanged horrified glances. Muriel's eyebrows twitched upwards.

One of the male guards stepped toward Eduardo and grasped his upper arm. "I'll show you out, sir."

Seriously?

"And you're coming with us, Vivian."

Vivian?

Eduardo struggled in the strong grip of his guard without success. "What is going on here? Unhand her. Let her go. What are you doing?"

But the male and female guards already had Vivie twenty feet away.

As I caught up to them, I heard the clang of metal on metal

and knew that Eduardo had been escorted out of Guilt-Land. I took a last look back to see Eduardo and Maria staring mournfully from the other side of the fence.

Muriel had remained on this side.

I heard the guard warn against touching the fence. I found myself wondering if an electrical charge would hurt more from the inside or the outside.

It seemed Vivie and Eduardo would be separated once again.

The building Vivie and I thought might be a restaurant or store, turned out to be a makeshift prison. We ascended the rickety back stairs to a short hall with, from what I could see, four doors leading off it. The female guard opened the second one on the left and motioned that Vivie should enter.

Vivie did and without further instruction or comment, the two guards brushed past me and left.

The room had a small single bed with a folded quilt laying across the foot of it, a dresser with a small mirror over it, and a wooden chair. A window looked out onto the street below and wonder of wonders, a door led out onto a balcony.

Assuming that the balcony simply *had* to be some kind of delusion or trick, I held Vivie back and took the first step out myself. It held. It was sturdy. Granted, the balcony railing had bars, which did give it that certain prison ambiance, but I could see no way of *not* escaping. Our problem would be the electrified fence. What was this place, anyway? They hadn't even locked the door to Vivie's… room? cell?

The unexpected comment from behind me made me jump. "Looks easy enough," said Muriel, unwrapping her robe. "Here. Tie a few knots in this and secure it to that bar."

I did as bidden and in no time, Vivie and I were on the street with our arms outstretched to catch Muriel's robe as it floated down.

"Nobody can see me, so I'll go out the way we came in,"

Muriel called down to us. She disappeared, but only for a moment. "I would recommend you don't take the same path between this building and the little house we came in on. Go around the other way. I'll meet you out back."

Vivie and I nodded at each other and followed Muriel's suggestion.

Around behind the building we went, but cautiously, and hid among the boxes and barrels there until Muriel arrived.

"Lucky we had that experience at The Mazes, aren't we?" she said as she untied two of the central knots in her robe to spread out the middle section. I knew she planned on somehow covering the razor wire with her robe. "Can you figure out the best way to do this, Sandra?"

"How about we disconnect the fence somehow before we try anything?"

"There's a shovel over there," said Vivie. "It's got metal on it. Would that do something?" It wasn't long before she had it in her hand and was heading toward the fence. I stopped her.

"Allow me."

"No," Muriel said. "Allow me."

Muriel stepped to the fence and placed her hand on it. Nothing happened.

"Head games. That's all it is. Head games to keep people in line and obedient to their insecurities. If you want to control people, make them feel guilty." She stretched her arm out to me. "Hand over my robe. Please."

It took maybe four tosses, but we managed to get Muriel's robe draped over the two rows of razor wire and hanging down on either side of the fence. Without too much difficulty, we were able to force a large knot at one end of her robe through the mesh of the fence to secure it. The part hanging down on the other side, we pulled through then knotted. Once over, we worked the knots out of the mesh, and Muriel's robe once more covered her corset.

No sooner was Muriel re-garbed than Vivie took off into the forest after Eduardo.

"Go ahead, Sandra. I'll be fine. I'll meet you folks later."

Forty-four

<u>Grudge-Land</u>

IT MUST HAVE BEEN ALL the running exercise I'd been getting lately, but I wasn't even out of breath when I caught up to Vivie who was still on the path that went through the forest. Well, not that out of breath, only enough to allow her the first question.

"What happened back there?" she demanded. "That was about as absolutely ridiculous a fake prison imaginable."

"Um. You didn't happen to have a fleeting desire—as in made a wish—to be separated from Eduardo, did you?"

"That's even stupider than that fake prison."

"Hey, hey, now. There's no need for personal attacks against me. I'm on your side, remember? You don't think I'd rather be somewhere else than tripping over tree roots in the bush with you? Ow. Slow down."

I thought her sudden stop in front of me was merely a sarcastic reaction out of her general anger at the entire universe and she was taking it out on me, but the look on her face when she turned around said otherwise.

"Do you think Eduardo made a wish to be separated from me?"

"Well, I've never been much good at reading minds, but I highly doubt Eduardo would wish you anywhere but beside him, especially in this place."

"It must have been Maria then." She resumed her speedy trek along the forest path.

"It wasn't me, that's for sure. You're a lot easier to handle when Eduardo's around."

"Why would Maria do that to us?"

That was a good question. It did, indeed, seem like a set-up. It was just too easy to get out of that so-called prison. Way too easy.

"Maybe Muriel had a hand in it? I can't imagine Maria separating you guys. That's just not necessary anymore. Did you know that?"

Either she didn't hear me, or was running my comments over in her head, because Vivie remained silent until we exited the forest. We stopped walking.

"Well?"

"Let's sit down for a minute. I'm winded."

She was winded. "Best idea you've had since I met you."

"Ha ha." She settled herself on a boulder about ten feet from the edge of what looked like, from this angle, another cliff.

I sat on the boulder across from her.

"I've been thinking. That Muriel person seems to show up at the most convenient and inconvenient times. Doesn't she? And there's a word that describes it better, but I can't think of it right now."

"Contrived, maybe?"

"Ah, the perfect way to describe it. Yes." She smiled and rose from her boulder to approach the lip of what turned out to be, not a cliff that we would once again need rescuing from— please, no—but an easy sloping hill down into what looked like, from here, some medieval village.

I couldn't help myself, I gasped. It was as though an artist had painted it. The village was circular with a high wooden fence around the entire perimeter except for a large wide-open gate at our end. The strangest thing was that every property, every home, had its own individual high wooden fence around it, too. Every neighbor was separated from every other.

"Vivie. Do those things on the roofs of the houses look like machine guns?"

"It looks like guns or something sticking out of some of the windows, too."

Occupying what one might call the town square—although in this case perhaps the term "the town round" might be better—were all kinds of churches, synagogues, mosques, temples, pagodas… I didn't even know the name of half of them, but they were all religious buildings. There were dozens. Each with their backs facing a beautiful common park with no walls or fences, just more of those exotic flowers I'd seen after our escape from Fear-Land earlier. The path with the beautiful flowers that would have led us here at *that* time if Vivie had not eschewed it in favor of seeking out Eduardo in Guilt-Land.

From this distance, it seemed every street and alley of the entire village was paved with marble. This except for the walkway encircling the village round, and the paths in the Central Park area that was full of blooming fruit trees, bushes and flower gardens. The view was spectacular, but the feeling was not.

"Why are those religious buildings in a circle like that?"

Was I joking when I replied? "Looks like a scene from an old John Wayne movie. I can almost hear him saying, 'Get them wagons in a circle, pilgrim.'"

Vivie's pinched brow told me she didn't know what I was talking about.

"Back in the old days, people—settlers—moved west in covered wagons. When they were attacked by the native people living there, apparently, they got their wagons into a circle."

Vivie's brow was still pinched.

"For protection. You know, so nobody could sneak up behind them."

I guess I wasn't explaining it well enough. Or perhaps she was puzzled that the settlers hadn't just turned around and gone back to where they came from. That idea had often crossed my own mind. Perhaps we would get a chance to discuss the subject later. Right now, we needed to get ourselves through Grudge-Land.

We made our way down the hill and through the opening in the high wooden fence.

From this angle, I realized that the wooden fences around the individual properties weren't as high as the main one, and I could see through the narrow slits, where their gates met their fences, that they were barred on the inside, some with as many as three or four bars.

"Real friendly place, isn't it?" I said.

"Ew."

"What?"

Vivie pointed to the marble walkway.

Ew, was right. It wasn't marble. It was stained concrete. Where had I seen that before?

"It's like that guy who didn't want any money, but he was begging. In front of that store."

"The *Cose* store. Joey."

She nodded.

"Where Joey dissipated."

Vivie moved her feet cautiously to an unstained spot, but around me the stains were so numerous, I had nowhere to step.

"Let's move over to the grass by the fence there."

She followed me.

Above us, stapled or nailed to the fences surrounding the properties—I couldn't make myself think of them as family homes—were posters warning:

STAY BACK.

GET AWAY.

NO SOLICITORS.

TRESPASSERS WILL BE SHOT.

Below us, on the grass, just where I was about to step, was a vicious bear trap.

This was worse.

"Come on, Vivie. Let's go to that building there."

Holding hands, and not daring to look down at the stains on the concrete, we ran to the nearest religious building intending to enter its open door.

I had thought Hiram's lynch mob was frightening.

A group of men—and perhaps women, too, it was impossible to tell because of the outfits they were wearing—barred our way.

"Halt." I couldn't tell from which person the voice had come, but it sounded female. I didn't want to stare because these dudes were all carrying huge guns, shields, and were wearing camouflage outfits, helmets and face coverings. The last thing I wanted to do was upset one of them.

I whispered to Vivie. "Is this what they call a SWAT team? They were after my time, but I've heard about them."

"Shhh."

The same voice demanded: "Whom do you worship? How do you worship? Why do you worship?"

"What does it matter?" Vivie responded. "And what business is it of yours?"

I nudged Vivie with my elbow but that did not deter her.

"Who are you people? My companion and I wish to enter this building."

One of the group stepped forward to point his or her weapon at me. "What companion? Are you mad?" It was the same voice, and it was female, and she indicated the building we had been heading toward. "No one mad is allowed into our building. Where is your building?"

"How am I supposed to know from the outside? These buildings are all the same to me."

Several in the group laughed, but not the woman with the gun. A second person stepped up beside her—this one was male, "I think she's lying. I think she's just pretending to be crazy. That means she belongs to one of those weird religions."

The woman replied, "Ah, like the one around the corner at the back."

Her companion replied, "Yeah, I can never think of the name of that one either. Who'd want to, eh boys? A bunch of crazy people belong to that one."

This one aimed his gun at Vivie. She was standing her ground. Good girl. I was very proud of her.

"Crazy how?" Vivie asked.

The woman answered. "They let everybody and anybody into their… What do they call their building, Popeye?"

"Popeye" shrugged and turned toward the rest of the group. Their gun belts rose and fell in the negative as well.

"Nobody knows," the woman said. "Nobody really hangs around anybody else here. We've never seen anybody in there, so there's never really been anybody to ask." She lowered her gun.

Behind her, Popeye lowered his gun, too. "Come to think of it, have you ever seen anybody in *our* church?"

A mutter rumbled through the group. From the back of the group, a second female voice spoke up. "I've never been in there and neither has my husband. We don't bring the kids here either."

"Same with me," Popeye said. "Mom and Dad have never been near the place. We don't go anywhere, ever. Maybe that's why I don't have a girlfriend or a wife."

A male on the other side of the group laughed. "You sure that's the only reason, Popeye?"

They all laughed at poor Popeye.

I wasn't quite sure they were as relaxed as they were sounding, so I stepped forward. I wasn't surprised no one acknowledged my presence. Confirmed then. These were residents. Permanent residents, so they couldn't see me. I knew, therefore, they couldn't hear me either, so I told Vivie it might be wise for her to saunter slowly away toward the open door of the building.

When she hesitated, I assured her nobody would be following her inside.

Wonder of wonders, she accepted my advice without argument, semi-curtsied a thank you to the group, and calmly walked away from them.

Once safely inside, she grumbled, "What a bunch of wackos."

"Ya got that right."

"I wonder if they do that to everybody."

"Do you care?"

"That's a good question. If everybody in this town is the same, I guess they deserve to be treated like that?"

"Well, I for one, am not going to judge anybody in this town. And I'm not going to, for *absolute* sure, hold a *grudge* against those guys."

We both laughed, I think more out of a sense of relief than because what I said was particularly funny.

I wasn't the least bit surprised, of course, to see that the building—it was a church—was empty of people. Near the far end on both sides of what was an elaborate altar, were statues of various saints and religious figures. The wall behind the altar was decorated with stone angels. On the right-hand side of this wall, an opening led out into what I knew had to be that lovely interior common park we had seen from the hill. I did not have to make any suggestions to Vivie.

Here in the park, a great peace seemed to float in the atmosphere. There were more of those exotic flowers here and they were even more luscious than the ones leading into the village. The back door of every building was either wide open or absent in the first place. There were no fences, no signs. Nothing separated one building from another.

I hadn't seen it from the top of the hill, but there was an empty space between two of the buildings. Let me rephrase that. It was a pathway—with no tree roots, I might add—through trees blooming with every color imaginable, with fruits and berries hanging from them, and birds and small animals flickering and skittering throughout. Think Walt Disney's *Bambi*, during the opening scenes.

"Want to try that route?" I asked Vivie.

She agreed, and taking my hand, allowed me to lead her through the pathway. Those exotic flowers were everywhere as was the scent of cinnamon and cloves.

A sudden flutter of flowers made me jump as a small brown creature with floppy ears hopped out and rose on its hind feet in front of Vivie.

"It's *Petunia!*"

Ever so gently, Vivie reached down to slide her hand under the rabbit's hind end to lift it up to cuddle in the curve of her neck. The rabbit pressed its head against Vivie and closed its eyes in ecstasy.

"Can we bring her with us?" she asked.

"Of course."

"It's Petunia. It's really Petunia."

"I know, honey. I know," I told her as I put my arm across her shoulders, taking care not to frighten or disturb Petunia. "We're almost where we need to be. See that light up ahead?"

"It's more of a shimmer than a light. What say we call it a glittering shimmer?" She moved Petunia from her neck to cuddle her against her chest. "She'll be able to come with me?"

"She will."

"Will you?"

"I think Pete might have another assignment for me. I don't know anything for sure right now. Right now, I have to get you through that… What did you call it? A shimmer. A glittering shimmer? Well said, o fellow writer."

Neither Vivie nor I had any idea what lay beyond the glittering shimmer, although I knew we both had a pretty good idea that it was the end of the road, the end of tests, the end of temptations and guilt and woodsmen and dudes in fleece jackets riding double-seater tricycles and lynch mobs and SWAT teams. For her, at least. I knew full well that Trevor a.k.a. Pete—or somebody like him—would have a new assignment for me.

"Are you ready for this?" I asked her.

Holding Petunia safely aside, she hugged me. "What's that old cliche? Ready as I'll ever be? Thank you, Susan. Thank you for everything."

I couldn't help myself I kicked at a stone on the ground.

Vivie grinned wide as she re-cuddled Petunia and said, "If you say 'aw, shucks ma'am' I'm going to have to report you for cruelty to your Charge."

We hugged again and off she went into the glittering shimmer.

As I turned away, somewhat sadly because I liked her and would miss her, along came Maria hauling Eduardo along with her and yelling, "Is it too late? How long ago did she enter?"

"Just now."

Forty-five

<u>The Border of Grudge-Land</u>

EDUARDO TOOK THE TIME TO hug me and kiss both my cheeks. "Thank you for everything."

He turned to hold Maria's face in both his hands. "You'll never know how much I appreciate everything you have done for me. I will never forget you."

"I will never forget you either. But go go go! Don't let her get too far ahead of you."

Eduardo ran into the shimmer.

I heard a Vivie giggle and a delighted male laugh.

"He made it," Maria said as she hugged me. Her strength had not diminished since I had last seen her.

"I'm happy about that, too."

"Listen, Susan. I'd love to hang around and see how all this works out, but I've been assigned a new Charge. Gotta go." Maria actually put the back of her hand to her forehead. "Never a dull moment, is there?"

Another hug and off she went along a path that led away and downward along the edge of the shimmering gateway.

"Break a wing," I called out after her. "Hey. Who is your new Charge? Or should I ask?"

"Thanks," she waved back. "It's Hiram. Can you believe it?

This should be interesting." She paused to point behind me. "Maybe even as interesting as that." And as she disappeared into the trees, with her customary guffaw, she got in the last word: "Have *fu-u-u-un*."

I hoped I was seeing things.

There were Muriel, Trevor a.k.a. Pete and, wonder of wonders, George. As a chorus: "Well done, Sandra."

"What is this? The three musketeers? No, wait. It's more like the Three Stooges."

George did his palms up thing which made me wonder again if he and Eduardo had ever hung out together. "C'mon. Be nice."

"You were all in this together?"

"Nice job, boys," Muriel said. "And you're right. She is a handful."

Everybody laughed but me.

To me, Muriel said, "You're with them now. Good job, Sandra."

"It's Susan."

Muriel stepped away and as she did, she morphed into a creature glowing so brightly, it was almost impossible to watch. Was she male or female?

Trevor called out to her. "Thank you for stepping in for me, Uriel."

George added: "Yeah, Uriel. Appreciate your not giving me away, eh?"

I asked, "Is she…? Is he…? Is that really…? What did you call her? Him? What is she? A her or a him?"

With robe glowing and impossibly huge, shining white feathers, Uriel faded into the sky.

"Does it matter?" Trevor asked, all smiles at me. "Did you hear what Uriel said? You're with us now."

One on each side of me, Trevor and George led me toward the path where Maria had disappeared, all the while arguing with each other.

"I want to be the bad boy goon leader this time, all right, George?"

"Aw. I only got to do that the one time. Can I not do it again?"

"C'mon. You have to share."

"But I don't like being the bossy know-it-all."

"Nobody does."

Teasing laughter.

"What are you guys talking about? You mean, the goons and the cheerleaders weren't real?"

"Nope," said George. "They were figments of your imagination."

"Even Joey?"

"Sadly, no. We, meaning me and Linda, had even teamed up to try to help him, but there was no way for him. He was stuck with the idea of worshiping a lesser god."

"That's too funny, George!" snickered Trevor. "A lesser god? You?" The snicker became a full-out laugh. "You're only a saint, not a god."

"Saint as in Saint George? Like Vivie thought?" I stopped walking.

George bowed and swept an invisible plumed Musketeer hat across the ground in front of himself. "One and the same." He twirled to come out of it in his suit of armor, but this time, sans sword and shield. Another twirl and he was back to being George the goonster.

"Enough of the jokes," he said. "I was very sad for poor Joey. We did our best. We really did."

"You and Linda did your utmost with him," said Trevor. "And I understand his last moments were somewhat peaceful?"

"Yes. Even though he knew it was the end of everything. Very sad. But experiencing the Second Death in Comfort-Land is better than being all alone and dissipating in Section Four, don't you think?"

"Excuse me," I called after them. I still hadn't budged and hadn't quite absorbed what they'd been talking about, I'd ask them later. Right now, I had a pressing concern. "I have another question. If you are the real Saint George… Then was that…? Was that Uriel? Like the *real* Uriel?" I pointed to the spot in the sky where Muriel a.k.a. Uriel had disappeared.

Without thinking anything special about it, as in no biggie, the boys agreed that yes, it was Uriel. "But he goes by many names."

"And he even goes without a name, too, if the occasion calls for it."

"Yeah." Trevor laughed and pointed at George. "Uriel had to pretend to be Beelzebub to get *your* attention. Remember?"

"Don't bring that up again."

I was gobsmacked, but Trevor brought me out of my daze. "You coming?"

I caught up with them.

Trevor slapped George on the back. "All right. You can be the bad guy goon leader again." Then he thumb-pointed at me. "And Sandra can be your gun moll."

They laughed.

"A gun moll? And it's Susan."

"Hey. Have we stumped Ms. Writer here on a film noir term?"

"I know what a gun moll is. It's a gangster's girlfriend."

"Exactly."

"Seriously? You seriously expect me to pretend to be a gangster's girlfriend? And the gangster will be George?"

"Seriously."

"Toad poop."

Acknowledgments

A VERY SPECIAL THANK YOU goes to Baileigh Binda, Phyllis Bohonis, Evelyn Crete, Cathryn Munroe, and Catina Noble.

About the Author